# VENETIAN BLONDE

---

## CHARLES BISHOP 3

### DAVE SINCLAIR

# VENETIAN BLONDE

**Bishop returns and nothing is as it appears.**

Off the coast of Norway an abandoned container ship is discovered, its crew slain, and the only clue is a photo knifed to a bulkhead. A photo of Charles Bishop with a note that reads, "It's all my fault".

Bishop leaps into an investigation that takes him from the frozen climes of Scandinavia, to the sun-drenched shores of Venice and the chaotic streets of Istanbul for a final fatal encounter.

With his own personal history catching up with him in the most violent way possible, Bishop will be forced to confront his past to save the present.

An all-out adventure with fast-paced dialogue and deception at every turn, *Venetian Blonde* is unputdownable.

# NOTE TO THE READER

**Although the Bishop novels can be read in any order, the events described in this book take place after those in** *Agent Provocateur***.**

*Dedicated to my mum and dad.*

*Thank you for your amazing support and always encouraging your two creative kids. Dad may have passed away a few years ago, but mum is forever supportive, even if her coffee table is now overflowing with books by her offspring. With love.*

# PROLOGUE

The wave pounded against the hulking cargo ship, which severely listed on the port side. On the bridge of the Norwegian Coastguard vessel *NoCGV Rolo*, the four-person bridge crew watched silently as the cargo ship was tossed about. Another wave like the last and she would be in danger of capsizing.

"Soon as the storm hits, that thing's going down." Captain Sørensen was a thirty-year veteran and had the cynicism to prove it. "They'll need to close the shipping lane."

Thunder clapped, making everyone but Sørensen jump. Helmsman Martinsen did his best to keep the huge cargo ship in sight. It wasn't easy. With no running lights, it bobbed up and down in the choppy Norwegian Sea. It was three am, and Martinsen hadn't been relieved in hours. The *Rolo* had been on its way back to port when they'd received news of an apparently abandoned cargo ship. The *Rolo* was tasked to investigate.

The radar showed the encroaching storm. The crew didn't want to be anywhere near the rudderless cargo vessel when it struck. It was predicted the storm would generate ten to twenty-metre-high swells, and rain so thick visibility would be down to virtually nothing. Even with the lack of sleep, Martinsen was having no trouble keeping his eyes open.

"What if there's crew aboard?" Erikson was the youngest crew member. She was also the newest, having only come on board three weeks earlier.

The crew watched another wave hit the big ship full on the stern, and it listed once again. It lunged down with a thunderous splash and they had to wait until the spray dissipated to confirm it had survived.

Sørensen raised an eyebrow. "No distress call. No flares. You're telling me if you were on that thing you wouldn't be doing everything you could to get off that deathtrap?"

"What if they can't?" It was the first time Erikson had ever stood up to the Captain. It was more terrifying than she'd imagined. "What if they're trapped, or out of power and out of flares? Wouldn't you want someone to come save you if you were on that ship, Captain?"

Behind the Captain's back, crewpersons Martinsen and Peppard reeled at that one. Erikson's one friend on the ship, Deb Peppard, shook her head and pursed her lips. She knew the Captain far better than Erikson and was sure he was about to explode.

"Have you seen the radar?" Sørensen pointed for effect. "The ship is rudderless. What if we board her and can't get the thing under power before the storm hits? Without it she's going down in the next thirty minutes. What exactly would you have us do, Sub-lieutenant Erikson?" Sørensen spat her rank like venom.

"If it sinks, they'll shut down the shipping lanes, the overboard containers will be a hazard for months and the clean-up will cost a fortune, not to mention the lost millions in transport delays. What would I do, sir?"

Erikson straightened her back and stared the Captain down. "I'd take an inflatable and board her now, sir. The gangway is down, it's possible. Once aboard I'll try and start the engines, get her out of harm's way. I can do it."

Martinsen's mouth dropped open. "You're insane."

Instead of agreeing with his helmsman, Sørensen smirked. "You really think you can board the vessel and get her started in time, Sub-lieutenant?"

Erikson didn't blink. "Yes, sir, I do."

The two stared at one another for the longest time. For Erikson, it felt like all air had been taken from the bridge. She was intimidated, but refused to show it.

Slowly, the semblance of a genuine smile formed around the edges of the Captain's mouth. "Take the inflatable. You wear thermals, GPS tracking, the whole kit. Soon as I get a visual on that storm you bug out without delay, you hear?"

Smiling, Erikson nodded. "Yes, sir."

"I can't figure out if you're amazingly brave or insane." Peppard shook her head.

"You'll be able to determine that firsthand, Peppard. You're accompanying her."

Peppard cast Erikson a pissed expression. "Why are we friends again?"

Erikson waggled her eyebrows. "Come on, we have a storm to outrun."

Lighting flashed, blinding Erikson for a second. A wave crashed against the bow of the inflatable and she lost sight of the enormous ship. She blinked several times as they crested a wave, and there it was. It wasn't on the horizon, it *was* the horizon. The vessel was colossal, it stretched as far as she could see. And they were getting closer.

"That's it!" she shouted to the Ensign driving the submersible. She didn't know his name yet. "Keep pace with the gangway, I'll let you know when to bring us in."

Beside her, Peppard seethed. "You better hook me up with that cousin of yours after this. You owe me."

"Where's your sense of adventure, Deb?" The wave rolled, bringing the two vessels closer. As the mighty ship swayed, the gangplank dunked into the sea. Erikson shouted, "Now, Ensign, now!"

The kid did as he was told and brought the submersible within a metre of the churning ship. Without a word being exchanged, both Erikson and Peppard leapt across the abyss onto the base at the end of the gangplank. Erikson landed smoothly, Peppard unsteadily. She teetered backwards, but Erikson grabbed her life vest and pulled her in.

Smiling, Erikson pushed her friend towards the long set of stairs. "Let's go!"

They had maybe twenty minutes before the storm would hit. The two were thrown against the railing, and had barely regained their footing when they were buffeted in the opposite direction. The massive ship was far from stable. They had to move. Wheezing, they made it onto the deck and took a moment to gather themselves. Out of breath, they exchanged hand gestures as the ship rocked. Peppard dashed for the engine room, Erikson the wheelhouse.

Making her way towards the superstructure at the rear of the vessel was like navigating a hallway while drunk. The floor kept moving and Erikson wasn't sure she'd keep her last meal down. But that wasn't the most distressing thing. She noticed small pockmarks on the deck. They didn't appear to be normal wear and tear damage; they looked like bullet holes. She did her best to dismiss the thought and forged on.

Two decks up, she encountered what appeared to be a barricade. Or at least, the remains of one. Bullet holes riddled the makeshift wood and steel barrier. It had clearly failed to provide protection; it was smashed apart. *What the hell happened here?*

Finally reaching the wheelhouse, Erikson saw that the main door was plastered with more bullet holes. The glass was smashed, and the door had been blown off its hinges.

Unarmed, Erikson gripped her Maglite and leapt boldly into the wheelhouse. There was no need for the theatrics. The wheelhouse was empty.

Erikson gripped the microphone strapped to her vest. "Deb? You there? Some weird shit's gone down on this ship."

There was no reply.

"Deb?" Erikson inhaled deeply. "Deb!"

"I'm... holy shit... I'm here. There's... holy shit..."

"Deb." A massive wave shunted Erikson to one side, and she braced herself against the wall, struggling to remain upright. "Deb, I need those engines."

"I... I... there's something down here. Lots of somethings."

"Deb, everything else can wait." Erikson watched a huge wave roll slowly towards the wheelhouse. It was the biggest one yet. "Now, Deb!"

"I... Okay, I think... Switching on now."

After several seconds, consoles blinked to life in the wheelhouse. Navigation, engines, everything came online.

Erikson clapped her hands in glee. "You're a miracle worker, Deb. Let me do my thing."

It took Erikson another ten minutes to get all the

ship's systems fully under power. In fifteen, they were steering away from the storm. The ship had been saved. Captain Sørensen congratulated them both and ordered them to steer towards the Port of Oslo.

Twenty-five minutes later, a pilot vessel arrived and relieved Erikson of the wheel. They would guide the big ship into port.

Now that steering the massive vessel was no longer her concern, Erikson contacted her friend. There was no immediate reply. She tried again.

When she eventually replied, Peppard's voice was grave. "You need to come down here, now."

Erikson made her way down the stairwells leading to the innards of the mammoth ship. She landed on the deck of the cargo hold and strode towards the engine room. Normally the cargo hold of a container ship would be borderline claustrophobic, full to the brim, but not here. Only one or two containers were stacked, where they should have been five or six high. Of those left, most were rusted or badly dinted from years of use. It was a floating junkyard.

To herself, Erikson asked, "What the hell is going on here?"

Peppard greeted her at the door to the engine room. Her face was deathly white. Behind her on the wall was some sort of note, but Erikson ignored it, focused on her friend.

"Deb, what's…"

She didn't answer, and instead burst into tears. Peppard was tough as they came, crying was the last thing Erikson had expected from her. She moved to step into the engine room, but Peppard grabbed her arm and shook her head.

Erikson nodded in acknowledgement, then gently moved her friend's hand off her arm and proceeded anyway. Stepping inside, she was immediately over-whelmed by the smell. It was horrifying mixture of faecal matter, blood and flesh. But the smell was nothing compared to the vision before her. One on top of the other, bodies were stacked three high. There were fifteen, maybe twenty corpses. The crew.

Erikson staggered from the bloodbath and joined Deb on the floor of the cargo deck. Hands on knees, she fought to hold back the bile in her throat.

Erikson turned to look at the note near the door. But it wasn't a note at all. It was a black and white photograph, stabbed to the bulkhead with a hunting knife. Curiosity outweighing fear, she walked towards it. It was a photo of a handsome blonde man. The headshot had seemingly been taken from a distance on a street. The signs around him were in English. Over the top of the photograph were hand-scrawled words.

Erikson's shaky hand reached for her radio. "Captain. You're going to have to call the police to meet us in Oslo."

"What's that, Sub-lieutenant?"

With a trembling voice, Erikson explained the horrific scene and the photograph.

"There's something else. The photo has a message, sir."

"A message?" The Captain sounded as shocked as she was.

"Yes, Captain." She inhaled deeply. "The photograph says this is all my fault and there's a name. It's signed Charles Bishop."

## CHAPTER ONE

The vans sped by so close he had to throw himself against the taxi or he'd have been run over. He paid them no heed. His attention was elsewhere. The attractive young Coast Guard officer waited for him to round the taxi, and greeted him with a warm smile.

The woman extended a hand. "Welcome, my name is Erikson."

"Good morning. I'm—"

"I know who you are, Mr Bishop." The young woman tucked a length of blonde hair behind her ear and gave him an elfin grin. "I was the one to call it in."

"I see."

The woman didn't relinquish her hold on his hand and studied his face intently. "You're more handsome in person."

"And you're incredibly insightful."

Realising she was staring, Erikson let go of his hand.

"Those vans seemed to be in a hurry." He watched the five of them speed down the pier and turn towards the port entry he'd come through.

"The coroner, I think. Just took away the, uh…"

"Bodies?" The young woman nodded solemnly. Bishop went on. "From what I hear there was really no need to rush. I doubt their condition will improve."

Erikson scowled, as if to say, *too soon*. The two strode along the massive pier in a quiet section of the Oslo port facility. The sun shone, but the morning air retained a chill. Behind them, massive cranes hefted containers while enormous ships manoeuvred into place. The two of them were rugged up against the cold. Even with the layers, Erikson cut a lovely figure in her dark blue uniform. While he'd had misgivings about the excursion to Norway, Bishop was beginning to think the trip may not be entirely wasted.

MI6 had been informed about the photograph via a general bulletin posted by Interpol. There had been much consternation at Secret Service headquarters, but little in the way of actual intelligence. Bishop's organisation seemed to be as in the dark as any other as to why his picture had been knifed to the inside of a derelict container ship. Why him? What exactly was his fault?

Erikson led Bishop towards where the container ship *Valkyrie* was moored. It had certainly seen better days. The ancient vessel was rusted, dinted and in desperate need of either a paint job or mothballing.

"It seems old."

The young Coast Guard officer tilted her head in agreement. "Pretty obsolete by modern standards. She'd be lucky to pass port inspection, I'd say."

Bishop grunted, taking in the massive ship. Ocean-going vessels weren't really his thing, unless it was a luxury yacht moored to a dock and there was a party going on. And even then he'd have a hard time telling starboard from port.

At the base of the gangplank sat an aged, disinterested police officer. He rested on a folding chair and looked somewhere between sixty and Cleopatra's older brother. It was what they called a sunset assignment. He ticked their names off a list of authorised visitors and gave their credentials a perfunctory glance. The old timer had a hard time seeing through his fishbowl glasses. Bishop doubted he'd be one of Oslo's top cops.

The two started their long journey up the gangplank. Erikson stopped after ten metres.

She gave Bishop a sideways glance. "Was this your fault?"

"The murdered crew?" Bishop shrugged. "Not that I'm aware of." Noticing that his answer didn't seem to sate the Sub-lieutenant, he went on. "Not directly, no. Not even indirectly, as far as I know. Although, with the universe as it is, who's to say I didn't cause it through some random butterfly affect? You know, the cascade of causation and all that. For all I know I instigated it when I bought a packet of crisps in Lisbon, or that time I stole a comb when I was nine."

Bishop realised he was rambling. If he were honest, he cared more for the company of his companion than he did the assignment. Erikson had asked a valid question: was he involved? He was sure he wasn't, and as a consequence he viewed the entire exercise as a waste of time. It was only his curiosity that drove him now.

Erikson squinted. "Who do you work for, Mr Bishop? My Captain wasn't supplied with that information."

"I work for the British government." He showed her his perfect teeth. "Are we able to board? I was told the police were still aboard."

"The forensic team completed their job hours ago. Hence the clearing of the bodies, I guess. Customs have been through too; nothing untoward, just empty containers. I find it most odd that you were just let through a police line, I must say."

Bishop didn't answer, just motioned for Erikson to keep ascending the gangplank. "Where was the ship registered?"

"Panama." Erikson turned and walked on. "Which doesn't say a lot. It's the most common flag of convenience country. Our authorities are trying to trace the company it's registered with."

"Tell them not to bother, it's a front corporation. The address is an abandoned laundromat and the names of its directors all belong to people who died at birth."

Stopping her progress, Erikson pivoted towards Bishop. "If you knew all that, why did you ask me where she was registered?"

Bishop smiled. "I was making small talk."

"Right." Her eyes narrowed. "Who did you say you worked for again, Mr Bishop?"

"I didn't. I gave a vague yet charming answer, and you didn't ask further."

"I'm asking now."

"And I'm being even more vague."

A faint scowl creased her forehead. "And far less charming."

She stomped up the remainder of stairs in silence. When they reached the top, Erikson sucked in air, but Bishop remained fresh as the morning.

The Coast Guard officer's expression turned grave. "I warn you, even though the space has been cleared, it still won't be pretty in there."

"I'm sure I can handle it."

Bishop went to step on deck, but Erikson thrust out a hand to stop him. "What's this about?"

Bishop shrugged. "No idea."

"Why are you here?"

"No idea."

She squinted. "Do you know anything?"

"I'm free for dinner."

Rolling her eyes, Erikson playfully pushed Bishop onto the deck "This way, Casanova."

To be honest, Bishop could sympathise with Erikson's reaction. He sounded flippant, but in actuality he had no idea why he was there. Yes, there'd been a picture of him at the scene, but as far as Bishop knew, a cargo hold of dead bodies in the middle of the Norwegian Sea wasn't his fault.

The photograph had been taken near his apartment. That was concerning. It had been taken with a telephoto lens, most likely from a vehicle parked on his street. So whoever took the picture knew where he lived. If it was a threat, why not take him out with a sniper's bullet? It would be far less effort, and would have meant Bishop didn't have to catch two connecting flights and travel economy. He really hated flying economy.

The next few minutes were spent in silence as Erikson navigated her way through the bowels of the ship. As they stepped onto the cargo deck the Coast Guard officer slowed.

"It's just beyond… the…"

Bishop placed a hand on her shoulder. "You don't need to go in. It's fine."

Frowning, Erikson shook her head. "I'm going in. It's just I need…"

"You take as long as you need."

To her credit, the Coast Guard officer steeled herself, then immediately ducked through the doorway. The cramped engine room reeked. The bodies may have been taken away, but nothing could remove the stench of death. Bishop breathed through his mouth, but it did little to counter the horrific scene.

Blood was splattered on all surfaces. The police had mapped the bullet holes and would have taken samples for analysis. None of it would bring the dead crew back to life.

"Where's the photo?"

"Out here." Erikson held a handkerchief over her mouth.

The two stepped back onto the deck of the cargo bay. Erikson pointed to the photograph. It had been dusted for prints, but remained in the same position Bishop had seen in his briefing pack at MI6.

"I wonder why they left this here?" He said it out loud, mainly asking himself.

"The police were asked by your... vague British government department to leave it in place until you arrived. You must be pretty important if you can impose yourself on local police procedures, Mr Bishop."

"I'm but a humble public servant."

"I've known you for all of ten minutes and I can already tell you are most definitely not humble."

Bishop accepted the observation with a tilt of his head and bent down to inspect the stabbed photograph. While the knife and photo were real, the signature was far from genuine. The handwriting didn't even remotely resemble his own. *Curious.*

His gaze travelled down the wall and to the right, further into the cargo hold. He walked five metres and sat on his haunches. Bishop hand-traced the patterns on the floor.

"Huh." He frowned. "These scape marks..."

"The what?" Erikson shook her head, confused.

"Over here, on the floor."

"You came all this way to... look at the floor?"

"Not originally, but now I'm here..." Bishop pointed. "The scrape marks. Were they here the first time you came here?"

Erikson huffed. "To be honest, I'm not entirely sure. I

was somewhat distracted by the piles of dead bodies. I notice small details like that."

Bishop sniffed the air. "Still smells awfully bad, doesn't it?"

Bemused, Erikson opened her palms as if to say, *so?*

"But they took the bodies away?"

Not waiting for an answer, Bishop nodded and took a pen from his jacket pocket. He poked a section of floor near the main bulkhead.

Erikson placed her hands on her hips. "Why are you so interested in the floor?"

"Because if you take a look at these scratches are deep, meaning something heavy caused them. And there are minute metal threads still here, meaning they were made recently."

"So? This is the cargo hold. Heavy things get dragged through here all the time."

"Through walls?"

"What?"

Bishop pointed. "See here, at the edge? The scrape goes under the bulkhead. Not to the edge of it, but *under* it. Meaning?"

Erikson blinked several times. "It's a false bulkhead?"

"Precisely." Bishop winked. "Want to find out?"

Re-entering the engine room, Bishop found a crowbar on a rack of tools. Wedging the implement under the wall, he heaved. A sliver of movement proved Bishop's theory right. Erikson caught on and found a lead pipe. Jamming it under the gap Bishop had created, the two were able to lift the false wall.

The gap widened. Bishop panted, "There's another room in here. Let's get some braces."

A few minutes later they had wedged supports in place and Bishop could slip under and take a look. Inside, the room was about two cargo containers wide. It was also full.

Bishop's mind whirred.

"What's under…" Erikson covered her mouth and nose. "Why is the smell stronger now?"

Bishop slid back under the false wall and stood. "We have to move." Not waiting for an answer, he ran from the cargo bay back the way they'd come in. Erikson's puzzled form followed closely behind.

"What's going on?" Erikson puffed behind him.

"The false hold wasn't empty." Taking three stairs at a time, Bishop yelled behind him. "Call the port authority. Tell them to shut everything down, the entire port. Nothing gets in or out. Tell security to get the details of those coroner vans and pass them on to the police to issue an all-points bulletin."

Erikson stopped climbing stairs. "What? What are you on about?"

Bishop sighed. "The bulkhead was fake, meaning something was behind it, yes? It's not empty now, and do you know why? It contains the dead crew."

"But… but…"

"Those speeding vans who were, in your words, 'the coroner, I think' were nothing of the sort. I'm guessing whatever was behind the wall is now in those vans. And the dead bodies they were meant to pick up are now where the stash was hidden. Got it?"

Erikson opened her mouth, but no sound came out. Eventually she said, "I… I don't have the authority for that."

"Well, try."

She did just that. Bounding up the stairs, the Sub-lieutenant shouted and cajoled as best she could. Now it was up to the port authority, but Bishop feared it was too late.

As he stepped into the sunshine, Bishop was even

more confused. If this was about smuggling, surely there were more subtle methods? And why the need to drag him into it?

Erikson's phone rang and she answered as the two crossed the sun-drenched deck. Confusion creased her face.

She held the phone out to Bishop. "It's for you."

"Me?" Erikson shrugged and Bishop took the phone. "Hello?"

"Miss me, lover?" A woman's voice. Sultry. Confident.

Bishop frowned. "I'm terribly sorry, you're going to have to be more specific."

"More specific... I tried to kill you. Several times."

Bishop placed his hand on his hip. "I'm terribly sorry, you're going to have to be more specific."

"It's Astrid, you ass."

"I'm terribly sorry—"

"Stop being a fucker, Bishop!"

Astrid Spencer. Of all people. How on Earth did she get Erikson's number? Bishop groaned. Of course she was behind whatever charade was going on.

"What can I do for you, Astrid?"

Erikson frowned, and mouthed the words, *Who is it?*

Bishop placed his hand over the phone's microphone. "Just a power-mad arms-dealing psychopath I used to know." On seeing the surprise on Erikson's face, Bishop added, "It's okay, she's in jail." Puzzlement creased Bishop's face and he removed his hand from the microphone. "You are in jail, aren't you Astrid?"

There was a tiny giggle from the other end on the line. "Oh, I was. But the arrangement just wasn't for me. It didn't take."

"Most people don't have a choice."

"I'm not most people."

"That much is certain. Is this a social call or do you have something on your mind?"

Her voice turned to ice. "Revenge."

"Oh, that's lovely. Anyone in particular, or just a general revenge type vibe?"

"You, specifically."

"I'm flattered. Was the thing with the ship completely necessary? It seems overly theatrical, even for you."

"Was it?" Bishop could hear the amusement in her voice. "How else was I going to lure you?"

"Lure?" Bishop stopped walking and his eyes darted around the port.

"Didn't I mention the worldwide bounty on your head? Oh, silly me. You're a dead man, Charles Bishop."

Bishop's hand slid around Erikson's waist and he steered her back towards the superstructure of the ship. Confusion dripped from every pore, but she followed Bishop's lead.

"What have you done, Astrid?"

"What every jilted lover would do in my position. I've put a price on your head, my love. Five million dollars. That's a nice round number, don't you think?" Her voice was gleeful. "Oh, by the way, what time do you have?"

Bishop checked his watch. "Nearly eleven."

"What an amazing coincidence. The bounty becomes active at eleven. Which is, let me see… in… three, two, one. Good luck, Bishop. You'll need it." The phone went dead. He handed it back to Erikson.

Before she had time to tuck it into her pocket, Bishop grabbed her hand and broke into a run. They reached the hatch just as it was peppered with gunfire. As he leapt through the doorway, Bishop glanced back to see four men firing carbine guns as they stepped off the gang-plank onto the deck.

They were here to collect the bounty.

Hyperventilating, Erikson held up her phone, her hand shaking. "I…" She swallowed, struggling to get the words out. "I can't get a signal."

Blocked. These guys knew what they were doing.

As Bishop ran down the stairs, he assessed his position. Unarmed, in an unfamiliar environment, with multiple heavily armed professional assailants snapping at his heels. No backup. The situation was dire.

As they rounded a set of stairs, Erikson struggled for breath. "The police officer?"

Bishop knew she meant the meant the dithery old man who had signed them in. "He's already dead."

Her face regained some colour; it may have been fear, it may have been anger, Bishop couldn't tell. "What the hell did you do to this woman?"

"The usual." Bishop shrugged. "Slept with her. Brought down her evil global criminal arms-dealing network. Had her arrested. Stole her pen."

"Right." She scrutinised his face. "You don't exactly seem upset by this sudden turn of events. Some might even say you're enjoying it."

"What sort of lunatic would enjoy be shot at by assassins?"

"I'm asking myself that very same question, Mr Bishop."

He ignored the bait. Bishop had an ambush to improvise.

# CHAPTER TWO

From his high vantage point, Bishop watched the mercenaries slink onto the cargo bay. The four men moved as one. No verbal commands were issued, only concise hand gestures. They were highly trained—ex-Special Forces, if Bishop was to guess. Wherever they came from, they were soldiers of fortune making dirty money, damn the cost. Bishop was there to ensure the cost would be very high indeed.

The mercenaries split into two groups, each taking a side of the cargo bay. It was a fair move. But what they should have done is ensured one team had the high ground. That was their first mistake.

Bishop waited patiently until the two leftmost mercenaries began to make their way towards his shipping container. It didn't take long. Beside him, Erickson lay flat on her back in the centre of the container's roof, motionless, too terrified to even breathe.

En route to their position, Bishop had grabbed the crowbar and lead pipe they had used to pry open the false bulkhead. Against carbines it wasn't much, but it would have to do.

When the footsteps came close, Bishop acted, leaping between the two mercenaries. He heaved the lead pipe down on the lead man's gun arm, shattering his radius. The big man dropped to his knees. Swinging the heavy weapon downwards, Bishop smacked the side of the man's head, crushing his skull. Not waiting for confirmation of the man's injuries, in a fluid movement Bishop attacked his comrade. The man swivelled to see the source of the noise, but too late. Bishop used the crowbar in his left hand to hook the back of the mercenary's head and yanked it forward, right into the path of the pointed lead pipe. The blow shattered the man's eye socket. As his hand darted towards the devastating wound, Bishop removed the man's hunting knife strapped to the man's thigh. The blade to the heart quietened the man's suffering. A slit to his companion's throat did the same.

The men's agonised screams had put paid to any semblance of stealth. Bishop tucked two pistols and the knife in the band of his jeans and slid the Beretta CX4 Storm over his shoulder. He scrambled to the top of the shipping container and waited.

Lying on her back on the roof of the container, Erikson stared wide eyed in shock at the blood splattered across Bishop's shirt. The woman was justifiably terrified. What should have been a simple escort assignment had rapidly descended into terror and death. It was a lot to comprehend on a Monday morning.

In an attempt to reassure her, Bishop grinned and whispered as quietly as he could, "Now I have a machine gun. Ho ho ho."

Confusion creased Erikson's face. She replied in a low whisper of her own, "What's with the Santa impression?"

Bishop frowned. "What's with the... Haven't you ever seen *Die Hard*?"

"I don't watch a lot of old movies."

"Old?" Bishop scowled. "I'm seriously reconsidering our dinner date."

"We were never going to have a dinner date."

"Weren't we?"

A mischievous grin crossed Erikson's lips. "Yeah, okay, maybe we were."

cheered her up ever so slightly, Bishop gave her a wink, then turned his attention to the mercenaries who were no doubt approaching and would be indifferent to his dining plans. Bishop closed his eyes and listened.

Two sets of footsteps, treading carefully. The sound echoed around the steel structure, making it difficult to determine a precise location. But one thing was certain: they were getting louder.

As he waited, Bishop couldn't help wondering why the men were here at all. There had to be more to it than Astrid's revenge. The false hold. The dead crew. The bounty on his head. Astrid's sudden appearance when she should have been in jail. None of it truly added up. It was like a riddle that made absolutely no sense. And was in Swahili.

Like the woman herself, there were many layers to this situation, and not all of it logical. Even when they were literally at one another's throats, Astrid had confessed her attraction to Bishop, as if they were kindred spirits, soulmates somehow pitted against one another. Delusional was an excellent way to describe her. Unhinged was probably better. All Bishop had to do was survive the next few minutes so he could start getting answers. Easier said than done.

Carefully, Bishop slid the two pistols out of his jeans. Carefully controlling his intake of air, he listened and waited. He didn't have to wait long.

The two remaining men approached from the opposite side to where the cries of their comrades had been so suddenly silenced. They advanced with more caution than their predecessors had.

There was an audible gasp when the first man saw his slain compatriots, then a rustle of clothing. Bishop took that as one of the mercenaries leaning down and checking for a pulse. That's when Bishop acted.

Rolling himself into position, high on the lip of the container, Bishop took aim at the man furthest from him. The man didn't do an upward sweep. He should have. He wouldn't make that mistake again. Bishop placed a bullet in his forehead.

He turned to the other attacker, whose reaction was far faster than his compatriot's, forcing Bishop to reel back and roll away as the upper portion of the shipping container was peppered with gunfire. Crouching, Bishop sprinted away from the line of fire to the end of the container and leapt. Landing on another container, further away from the mercenary, Bishop didn't break stride and continued his above-ground run. He leapt onto two more containers. Heavy footsteps followed his course, leading the man away from Erikson. The only trouble was, Bishop was running out of containers.

The odds may have bettered, but he'd lost the element of surprise and worse, the hunter had become prey. There was one more container ahead, then beyond that, a solid bulkhead. Bishop swore. Sometimes his cleverness bit him in his well-shaped arse. Bishop leapt to the cargo bay floor and rolled. Standing with his back to a container, he waited.

The footsteps grew louder, but the echoes made it impossible to pinpoint the man's exact position. Doing his best to remain quiet so he could hear the encroaching assailant, Bishop silently extracted one of the pistols. Moving slowly so as to not make a noise, he tossed it to the end of the cargo bay, to catch the attention of the mercenary.

There was an audible sigh.

"The old throw a thing to make a noise to confuse the enemy, eh?" The man's accent was thick. Nordic. "What's next, a cat jumps in an alleyway? We have a car chase and crash into some boxes? I saw you toss the gun, moron." Bishop heard a pistol hammer being pulled back. "You're finished. Over the next few hours you're going to pay for what you did to my team. You have nowhere to run, little man."

Bishop aimed the carbine at the mercenary's back and fired. While the man had been talking, Bishop had made his way around the container, his. The assailant collapsed dead.

"You talk too much."

Bishop made his way back to Erikson on the top of the container, aware that more assassins could appear at any second. The young woman was huddled in the foetal position, shivering.

"Hey, hey." Bishop tried to sound as calming as possible. "It's over. They're gone. We can go." He extended a hand. The terrified Coast Guard officer looked up in surprise. He took her for a strong woman, able to handle herself in normal circumstances, but these circumstances were anything but normal. Bishop repeated himself. "It's over."

But Bishop was lying. It wasn't over. Not for him. It had only just begun.

❧

"This is eleven kinds of bullshit."

The limousine motored down the tree-lined lane as mottled sunlight shone through the leaves. The scene was picturesque. At least, it would have been if Bishop wasn't fuming.

Beside him in the back of the back of the government car, Bishop's boss, Paul Cavendish, smirked. "It's for your own good."

Crossing his arms, Bishop sulked. "I recall hearing the same thing when I was a teenager, but no good ever good came from learning the clarinet."

"There's a worldwide price on your head. Every dark web dirty job noticeboard, terrorist cell in need of cash and unstable wannabe-soldier of fortune is after your hide. Believe me, this safe house is the best place for you right now."

"The best place?" Paul hefted an eyebrow and Bishop realised he'd raised his voice. He swallowed his anger and calmed himself. It would not do to lose one's temper with one's supervisor. "If it was the best place it would have a pool bar with cocktails that taste like foreplay, but it doesn't, does it?"

"I don't know about the cocktails, but there is a table tennis table. Although there's just one bat, and the only ball has a crack in it."

"And the pool with a bar?"

"I believe there's a bird bath and half a bottle of expired cough medicine."

Bishop squinted. "You're loving this, aren't you?"

Paul held a splayed hand across his chest in mock shock. "My dear Charles, whatever would give you such an abhorrent idea?" He grinned far too broadly for Bishop's liking. "I'm only wondering how the mighty action man that is Charles Bishop will survive sitting still for more than five minutes."

Bishop returned his friend's smile. "I'll escape."

"We have guards for that."

"Aren't they meant to be protecting me?"

"Normally, yes." Paul leaned forward. "But I have met you."

Bishop folded his arms and decided to double-down on his sulking. It had only been eight hours since his run-in with the mercenaries in Oslo. He and Erikson had made it out of the port without encountering any more assassins. When he'd informed MI6, he'd been told to report straight to the airport. He'd promised the traumatised Erikson he'd return to take her to dinner as soon as he could, which seemed to lift her spirits. A specially commissioned private jet flew him out of the country.

Touching down at Farnborough Airport, he was met by Paul and the government car. From there they made their way to their current location of rural Selborne. It was a quiet part of the English countryside, far away from all the things Bishop enjoyed. His sulking reached an unprecedented level of intensity.

Already knowing what the answer would be, Bishop asked anyway. "What about my mission to Turkey?"

"Off, I'm afraid. Well, for you."

Keeping his eyes on the passing scenery, Bishop huffed. "Who're you putting in as mission commander instead?"

"David Lanaway."

Bishop's head snapped around. "That pretentious twat?"

"I think you meant to say fellow operative."

"That fellow operative pretentious twat?"

Paul sighed. "He's perfectly capable—"

"Of screwing the entire mission, I know. Hence the pretentious twat remark. You can't be serious. That... operative couldn't find Russia if you parachuted him into the centre of Moscow. You may as well scrub the entire mission—"

"Until you come back? Is that what you were insinuating in a most oblique and subtle manner?"

"Am I that transparent?"

"Like lensless glasses." Paul shook his head slowly. He had the headmaster routine down pat. "Believe it or not, the Service can survive without you. We have more than one person capable of leading a mission. At least two, at last count. The Turkey operation is no longer your concern."

Bishop had spent considerable time preparing for the mission, preparing his team and gathering background intelligence. Now he had to let another operative lead his team instead. Knowing it was a lost battle with Paul, Bishop's sulking took on a hitherto unknown intensity.

Yousef Sharif was the eldest son of the King and Prime Minister of Saudi Arabia. He had gone missing from public view three weeks prior in mysterious circumstances. Sharif was not only being groomed as a future leader, he was also a vocal member and head of the OPEC Board of Governors. Then he went missing. Kidnapped, executed, eloped? No one knew. The Saudis had offered a reward for his safe return. Then a few days ago he'd been spotted by an informant in a market in Istanbul with what appeared to be heavy security. The informant was a local Bishop knew well and trusted. The heavies had curtailed Sharif's movements and interactions with others, indicating that he wasn't free to come and go as he pleased. MI6 were interested in his wellbeing. There was an OPEC meeting in less than a week, which many believed could raise the price of oil significantly, unless cooler heads prevailed. Sharif was one of those cooler heads. That, combined with the increasing likelihood of a Russian civil war, suggested the world was on the brink of tumbling somewhere calamitous.

It was MI6's assessment that Sharif had been

kidnapped to sway the OPEC vote one way or the other. A primary remit of MI6 was to safeguard the economic wellbeing of the United Kingdom. If the leader of the OPEC board and the next in line to the throne of the second-largest oil producer in the world was kidnapped for economic gain, the ramifications could be enormous. The clock was ticking, and every delay meant the trail became colder. Bishop was pissed he'd have no part in an operation he'd invested so much in. He knew he'd have to get used to the idea, just as he knew that wouldn't happen any time soon.

The car turned off the B road and headed down what appeared to be an infrequently used side road, possibly last used during the civil war. After another five minutes they turned into a gap between high hedges onto a gravel road. As the car pulled up the drive, Bishop saw his lodgings for the foreseeable future: a large, well maintained, Tudor cottage. The grass surrounds were immaculate, as was the garden. Not far from the house was a large white wooden garage, the sort you'd expect to house a couple of Jaguar E-Types. It could have been the home of one of the minor members of the House of Lords.

Without a word, the two men exited the vehicle. Paul opened the boot and handed Bishop a bag he'd put together after visiting his apartment.

He tilted his head. "The clarinet. Really?"

Bishop shrugged. "Don't be fooled. It's not the chick magnet everyone claims it to be."

They were met at the front door by Jenkins, an officious ex-Scotland Yard detective in charge of security. He had all the humour of a mortuary owner's wake. Jenkins showed them around. The inside of the cottage had been fully renovated. There was a sun-drenched conservatory, a library and satellite TV. It was a beautifully appointed safe house. Anyone would love to be holed up there.

Except Bishop.

After Jenkins left them alone in the conservatory, Paul motioned for Bishop to sit. There were two luxurious leather sitting chairs, an ornate Indian-style coffee table between them.

Paul wiggled into a comfortable position. "This is nice, isn't it?"

Bishop turned to his boss. "I still don't know why I couldn't hide out in my apartment."

Paul's tone was matter-of-fact. "Because you'd be dead, that's why."

Bishop tilted his head. "My cooking's not that bad."

"Funny. It may interest you to know that MI5 picked up two lots of assassins breaking into your apartment in the last four hours. Armed to the teeth and ready to do you quite a bit of damage. A third team was picked up in a car nearby. No weapons present, but they're still being held for questioning, given they were in possession of your picture and were staking out your abode." Paul sighed. "So, you'll forgive me for taking some precautions with regard to your wellbeing. Make no mistake, there's a price on your head and many are looking to collect."

Bishop frowned. The situation was more serious than he'd thought.

Paul slapped him on the arm. "That's how I was able to get into your apartment and grab this." He pointed to Bishop's overnight bag. "Your front door was kicked in. The landlord's replacing it, by the way, but he did mutter something about raising your rent."

"Right." Realising he wasn't getting anywhere, Bishop changed the subject. "How's Nancy?"

"Oh, my beloved is just peachy. Fit as a fiddle. I think I've mentioned her Australian friend, haven't I? Lovely girl—completely mental, but lovely. She's in a spot of bother. Nancy, in her inimitable style, is trying to help, bless her."

Bishop was only half listening; he had a completely different topic on his mind. Jenkins appeared with a tray that held a pot of tea and some biscuits.

Paul whooped. "Jammie Dodgers. You are being looked after, my son. I'm lucky to get digestives at Vauxhall Cross."

Jenkins left and Paul poured.

"How did this happen, Paul? Astrid was arrested. I was there."

"Yes.

"And taken away by the police."

"She was."

Bishop was becoming agitated by Paul's aloofness. "She shouldn't be able to call in assassinations."

Paul handed him the cup and saucer. "Quite. Unfortunately, the arrest by the Haitians wasn't as clean as Interpol would have liked. She had the best lawyers the most successful illegal arms dealer on the planet could afford. She beat the charges, I'm afraid."

Bishop sipped. "Knowing Astrid, I wouldn't credit her legal staff entirely. I'm sure there were bribes and coercion on all sides."

"We're on the same page there. We're looking into it."

"It's a bit late. When exactly were you going to tell me she was free? My funeral?"

Paul frowned. "Don't be absurd. I'd never get through the throng of weeping trollops." His expression hardened. "I found out she was free when you did."

"Slightly after, let's be honest. I had to get through all the shooting and stabbing first."

"Fine, slightly after you." Paul smirked and poured milk. As he stirred, he eyed Bishop. "You'll be fine here, won't you? We have every available agent on this. We'll track her down, Bishop, I assure you."

He didn't believe it. Astrid would be a ghost. The woman knew how to cover her tracks and become invisible. If she didn't want to be found it would be impossible for any intelligence agency to track her down. Unless they had Bishop. He was the only one who'd met her and lived. Well, almost the only one. There was one other.

Pouting his lips, Bishop gave a near-convincing nod.

"Charles Bishop." Paul placed the teacup on the coffee table and leaned forward. "I know sitting on your hands goes against every fibre of your being, but I need you to solemnly swear as an Englishman and a gentleman that you will not do anything rash or stupid."

"When have you ever known me to do anything rash or stupid?"

"Constantly. I have an extensive list. That's not hyperbole, I actually have a list." His boss scowled. "I need you to listen to me, Charles—as a friend, I'm imploring you. There are countless assassins out for your head. I'm asking you for once in your stupid life to sit this one out. We're not neophytes here, we know what we're doing. We'll get her, and we'll cancel this damn contract. You'll be back at work in no time, but only if you stay put." Paul checked his watch. "Damn. I have a meeting with the Foreign Minister at three." He stood and extended his hand. "Good luck, I'll visit as much as I can." Paul leaned over Bishop. "And I mean it. I need you to stay put. Can you at least try?"

Bishop shook his hand. "Thanks Paul, for everything."

His superior eyed him closely but said nothing more, and left Bishop in the conservatory. As he watched the plain government car drive down the gravel path, Bishop tapped the arm of the chair restlessly.

"Well, I tried."

Bishop stood and started planning his escape.

The guards' routine was predictable. The two perimeter guards walked the boundary of the leafy property in sync, so one was opposite the other at all times. Jenkins and another officer were on house duty, the former patrolling the interior while his counterpart patrolled the garden path circling the mansion. It took Bishop all of ten minutes to find holes in their procedures.

While Jenkins clomped his heavy combat boots through the front parlours, Bishop found the staffroom. A set of Mercedes keys hung on a hook by the door. Pocketing them, he headed for the side entrance, closest to the garage. There he waited for the guard walking the nearby path to pass, and through a crack in the door he kept an eye on the boundary guard in the distance. The two disappeared from view at the same moment. Bishop quietly opened the door and walked briskly to the garage.

He was sure MI6 was doing all it could to find Astrid. He was equally sure it wouldn't be enough. The woman had forged the most successful illegal arms empire the world had seen, all while remaining completely anonymous. His organisation would be utterly incapable of tracking her down. Bishop knew her better than anyone in MI6. He knew her intimately.

He'd seen her at her most blissful, her most vulnerable, her most sadistic. He'd seen her masks, and her true face when they were removed. He'd seen what drove her, and what instilled her with fear. Bishop *knew* her. That was why he was the only one capable of taking her down.

The two of them shared the strangest of bonds. Part attraction, part hatred, part shared-soul, it was hard to describe. Astrid had attempted to kill Bishop several times, but even after all that, she acknowledged their unnatural attraction to one another. Bishop would say she was unhealthily obsessed with him, if not for the fact that he felt the draw as well.

No, Bishop could not leave the hunt to others. It had to be him.

Bishop slipped through the door without turning on the light. The garage was virtually pitch black, except for a sliver of light from under the roller door. Contrary to his initial thoughts, there were no E-Types, just a late-model Mercedes. Using the remote key to unlock it, Bishop jumped in the front seat, then poked around for the remote to open the garage door.

"Looking for this?"

The voice from behind him startled Bishop so much he jumped and his elbow hit the car horn. He swivelled and glared at the big man in the back of the vehicle.

"Jesus, you almost gave me a heart attack, you bastard."

"It's not generally advisable to refer to one's superior as a bastard."

Paul's face was a mixture of amusement and professional detachment. Quite the balancing act.

Bishop regained his composure. "I thought you had meeting with the Foreign Minister."

"I thought you promised to stay put."

Bishop frowned. "I never promised, I sort of talked around the subject."

Paul nodded. "I said I had a meeting with the Minister at three, I simply neglected to specify what day." He smiled. "With this level of deception we should be working for MI6."

"So you were waiting in the car in case I decided to make a break for it?"

"No. I sat here waiting for the moment *when* you would make a break for it. And I didn't have to wait long at all, did I?" Paul's face turned grave. "All frivolity aside, this just isn't cricket, Charles. We put you here to keep you alive. His Majesty's government is paying a hefty sum to keep your stupid head attached to your body. I know it goes against your very nature, but for once in your miserable life, follow orders and stay bloody put."

There was no arguing. Paul wasn't only right, he also held all the cards. His concern carried a veiled threat: do as you're told or your career is at risk. Bishop nodded and exited the Mercedes and the two strode back to the house. They passed a fuming Jenkins, who stood with his arms folded. Bishop gave him a couple of finger guns.

"While I was waiting in the car," Paul opened the door and ushered Bishop in, "I received a message from MI5. Mossad gave them a heads-up that two of their former employees were making their way to the UK to collect the price on your head. They were collared at Heathrow twenty minutes ago. This is what we're up against, Charles. Not a bunch of Army Reserve rejects with the afternoon off. These are professional killers with a CV that'd make Genghis Khan look like Gladys the tea lady. You need to stay here until we say otherwise." Paul led Bishop back to the conservatory. "I do hope we won't be having this conversation again."

"I can assure you, Paul, we won't be."

Bishop was telling the truth. He still had the keys to the Mercedes in his pocket.

# CHAPTER THREE

The Mercedes hummed along the rain-soaked A2. The car was a pleasure to drive. Or at least, it would have been if Bishop's mind hadn't been elsewhere. He was officially on the run from an unknown number of professional killers, and now his own organisation, too.

It was a little past two in the morning. Jenkins and the other guards were well behind him, and the headlights shone down an empty highway. His path was clear.

There was a heavy burden of guilt on his shoulders, having deceived and directly disobeyed his superior and friend, but this was Bishop's only choice. No one else could bring Astrid down. No one else knew her as he did.

He'd visited a twenty-four-hour storage facility outside of Dartford that he'd loaded up years before for this type of eventuality. On the seat beside him lay a bug-out bag, fake passports, a burner phone and identity cards. He'd also swapped the number plates on the Mercedes. It wouldn't be enough. Cut off from his own government, Bishop would need outside help to find Astrid. He needed intelligence.

With a deep sigh, Bishop reluctantly dialled the number.

After three rings a groggy voice answered. "Кто это?"

"It's Charles Bishop. I need your help."

"иди нахуй ежа" Bishop was well versed enough in Russian to know the phrase was roughly the equivalent of "go fuck a hedgehog".

"It's about Astrid."

There was heavy breathing down the line. Eventually, the thick-accented Russian replied, "Where are you?"

The Marco Polo Airport arrivals lounge overflowed with happy, excited tourists. The dull sunlight shone through the glass ceiling. Bishop wasn't nearly as excited, nor bright. He brooded over his bloody mary and watched the throng of energised commuters pass before him.

From Dartford, he'd made his way to the nearby Ebbsfleet International train station. He abandoned the Mercedes in a long-term car park, paying a month in advance. From there he took the Eurostar through the Channel Tunnel to Brussels, another train to Berlin, then a flight to Sarajevo, onto Rome and finally Venice. It was an awful, meanderingly indirect route, but it significantly reduced Bishop's chances of being tracked.

The bloody mary did little to wash out the appalling spate of travel coffee he'd drunk in the past thirty-six hours, and the lack of sleep did nothing to improve his mood. Every moment had been spent looking over his shoulder, wondering which passenger was a hired killer. His nerves were frayed and his eyelids fought a losing battle for rest.

The man he was to meet was neither a friend nor an ally. They had worked together, albeit reluctantly, only once before. It had not been a pleasant experience for either of them. In fact, the last time they had seen one another had not ended on good terms. The thought brought a grin to Bishop's tired face.

Their one joint mission had been a tense and tenuous partnership between MI6 and the SVR. They had been tasked with tracking down the mysterious and powerful illegal arms-dealing organisation known as Kali and its shadowy leader, Kuolema. That mission had brought them together—in more ways than one—with Astrid. They had shared her captivating company, and even a bed with her. At the time they believed she had been innocently involved in events, not the one orchestrating them. When it was revealed who she truly was, she had made them pay dearly for their naivety.

The man wasn't difficult to spot in a crowd. Dressed like a Minsk factory worker, he towered over the casually dressed tourists searching for the exits. Some women would consider him ruggedly handsome, others ruggedly intimidating. Bishop merely considered him a means to an end.

The big Russian made his way to the bar. On sighting Bishop, the SVR officer, from Russia's equivalent to MI6, strode over and glowered.

Pushing himself up from his stool, Bishop extended a hand. "Oleg, always a pleasure."

Oleg ignored his hand. "Last time we met you stabbed me in the leg."

"Don't be dramatic. It was only an ice pick."

"It required six stiches."

Bishop shrugged. "It was a fair exchange. You stole the only weapons we had and left me for dead in the most dangerous place on the planet."

Unswayed, Oleg growled, "I should stab you where you stand."

"Ah, but then I'd be less inclined to buy you a drink."

Motioning for him to sit, Bishop waved over the bartender and pointed at Oleg. The Russian ordered a Heineken and when Bishop wasn't forthcoming, handed over some euros. The bartender left to get the beer.

Oleg snorted and shook his head. "I thought you were buying me a drink?"

"I said I was inclined to, not that I actually would." Bishop leaned over and added conspiratorially, "I still hate you."

"That is one thing we agree on, Englishman."

The beer arrived and both men sipped their drinks for a time. Using Oleg to find Astrid was a risk, but Bishop's options were severely limited. He needed SVR's intelligence network, and Oleg was the only man capable of providing it.

Oleg finally broke the silence. "Why me?"

"Besides the fact I missed you dearly?"

"Besides that."

"You're one of the very few people on this planet who has met her, knows her true nature and is still breathing."

Oleg said nothing for a time and took another swig of his beer. "There is more you are not telling me."

"There always is."

"Nyet. There is something else besides spy business." He paused as a couple of garishly dressed tourists passed close by, and waited until they were out of earshot. "My communications department has confirmed she escaped justice. I was not pleased by this news. But this is not enough for you to contact me. There is more. Why not use your fancy, overpaid MI6? This is suspicious, I think. You tell me the truth, or I return to Moscow on next flight."

"I'm wondering why you're not still in Moscow, Oleg? Shouldn't you be protecting your own government or something? Last I heard, your country was about to topple into civil war. You didn't need to come here at all."

"I have reasons." He folded his arms. "Why are you here, *really*, Englishman?"

"Let's just say this is a less than sanctioned mission. It's personal." Bishop exhaled loudly. "She put a hit out on me."

The roar of laughter from the Russian made many people turn in his direction. When finished, he wiped away a tear. "Oh, that is priceless."

"It's really not. It has a price of five million."

A frown creased Oleg's forehead. "Why just you? We both took down her empire."

Bishop smiled his girl-slayer smile. "I suppose I made more of an impression on her."

"You know…" the Russian tilted his head, "you know this is not a good thing, da? That she singled you out?"

"I do."

"Well, perhaps you should not be so smug about it?" Oleg shook his head and took another swig, draining the bottle. "Only pretty boy Charles Bishop would take pride in being the target of assassins. You really are an idiot."

"Look," Bishop rubbed his eyes, "we could sit here all day exchanging unpleasantries, but we have other matters to attend to. Why are we in Venice?"

The Russian had been elusive as to why they were to meet in that particular city. He had only supplied a date and time, and scant little else.

It was Oleg's turn to appear smug. "Because Russian intelligence is the best in the world."

"There are some who may take umbrage to that."

The Russian waggled a finger at Bishop. "If you wish to know why we are here, you must first admit Russian intelligence is best in world." He folded his arms.

Inhaling deeply, Bishop sighed. Knowing the stubbornness of the man beside him, there was only one response. "Fine, Russian intelligence is the best in the world." Under his breath he added, "If you're a big Russian twat."

Ignoring the dig, Oleg went on. "The great and glorious SVR has learned that Venice is her birthplace. Astrid was born here."

Bishop hunched his shoulders as if to convey, *so what?*

"Her father is still alive and lives here." He pulled out a small piece of paper. "And I have his address. And up until our little intervention which brought her empire to an end, he was receiving a monthly stipend from Kali, meaning she still cared for the man and was in contact with him." Oleg waved the piece of paper in front of Bishop's face. "Now, I will need you to state without sarcasm how Russian intelligence is the best in the world."

Bishop motioned for the bartender to come over. "Excuse me, do you by any chance have an ice pick I could borrow?"

The water taxi bounced on a wave and sea spray flew into the air. Even under overcast skies, the approaching city was no less beautiful. Not that Oleg appreciated the view. As soon as they left the airport dock he'd thrown himself inside the cabin and groaned.

Below deck, Oleg clung to a life vest and looked positively green. Every wave elicited a moan and a fight to keep his lunch down.

The big Russian glanced at his watch. "We should have," he fought to keep himself from retching, "been there by now."

Bishop nodded. "True, but I gave the driver an extra

twenty to take the scenic route." He smiled sweetly as Oleg glared. "You're welcome."

Oleg looked ready to tear Bishop's arms off, if only he could keep from vomiting.

Before the Russian could reply, the captain yelled, "We're almost there, gentlemen. This is the Grand Canal. Calle Corner Piscopia O Loredan is not far."

Within a minute, the boat entered the canal and the movement of the boat became less choppy. Oleg slowly became a slightly lighter shade of green.

Sitting on the bench seat, Bishop folded his arms. "Why are you here, Oleg?"

"Because you are sadistic and paid the driver extra to torment me."

"Not the boat, Borscht Brain. Why are you in Venice? Given your love of boats, it seems an ill-conceived choice."

Oleg's face hardened. "I have a score to settle with this woman."

"You and me both. But all you had to do was send me the address. You didn't need to come along."

"Yes, I did. That woman tried to kill me, several times. She sold arms to the enemies of my people. She has caused the deaths of thousands of Russian troops in the Crimea, all because of her greed. Weapons tied to Kali killed troops of the 31st Guards Air Assault Brigade while they slept in their beds." His words faltered. He swallowed to compose himself. "Many were friends of mine. They were like brothers. They would be alive today if not for that woman. She is evil and needs to be removed from the face of the earth. That is why I am here." Oleg waggled a finger. "And to answer your point, I am not," he put on a terrible fake English accent, *"coming along too."* Oleg scowled. "This is my mission. I will find her. I will deal with her. You are only here because I allow it." He took a steadying intake of air, colour returning to his face. "You are my scrappy sidekick."

"I'm no one's sidekick, Oleg."

He tilted his head. "Nyet? Then why do you need my help, Englishman? Because you have been booted from MI6, I think, da? They finally realised you are too pretty to be a spy? I think this is very much the reason, hmmm? It is my organisation's intelligence-gathering expertise that has got us this far, therefore this is my mission."

"It's not, Oleg. It's really not."

"No?" Oleg pulled the piece of paper from his pocket and screwed it into a ball. Keeping an eye on Bishop, he opened the window to the cabin and tossed it into the canal. Oleg's hand went to his mouth in fake shock. "Oh, how careless of me." He grinned. "Now, admit you are my scrappy sidekick or you will never find the woman you seek."

"This is childish."

"*You* are childish."

The captain popped his head down. "Are you two alright down there?"

Oleg raised a challenging eyebrow. Bishop rolled his eyes at the Russian.

"Fine. I'm your scrappy sidekick."

"Ha!" Oleg bounced in his seat. "I never thought you would say it. Too amusing."

"You must be very pleased. Now can we go see the father?"

Oleg pulled a pistol from his jacket. How he got it through customs, Bishop had no idea.

"Da." Oleg checked his clip and slapped it into place. "Let us go see Astrid's father."

~

The weathered lane of Calle Corner Piscopia O Loredan was like any other in Venice: a thin, winding rabbit warren of crisscrossing streets with the occasional wrong turn into a canal. Bishop had been to Venice on multiple occasions, and even though it was a relatively small island, the confusing layout meant navigating the labyrinth was hit and miss at best.

He and Oleg clomped down the well-worn street looking for the right address. The numbers seemed to jumble about, and possessed little in the way of logic.

"Here it is." Oleg stopped in front of 4146.

Outwardly, the residence didn't appear to belong to a well-to-do recipient of illegal arms trade money. The battered door was surrounded by damaged brickwork, which from waist down grew steadily worse until at ground level there was little left but silt. The pleasures of Venice floods took their toll on all buildings.

"Let me do the talking." Oleg's demeanour was all business.

"Yes, boss," Bishop replied, words dripping with sarcasm.

Oleg knocked on the dilapidated door and waited. On receiving no answer, he tried again, louder. The third set of knocks almost took the door down.

Over the noise echoing back from the Grand Canal, Bishop could hear movement inside the apartment. The ancient door creaked open, and an old man shielded his eyes from the sunlight. Likely in his mid-fifties, he could have been much older. The lines on his face showed a lifetime of hard knocks and tough breaks. Bishop could see no resemblance to the angelic Astrid.

"Mr Spencer?" Oleg's tone shared Bishop's scepticism.

"Yes. I'm Alistair Spencer. What's this about?" The voice didn't match the weathered exterior. Definitely

English, with an aristocratic twinge. That matched Astrid to a tee.

"We were wondering if you were the father of Astrid Spencer."

The old man sighed. If it was possible, he seemed even older. "Right, come in then." He disappeared into the darkness of the apartment.

Oleg and Bishop exchanged glances and followed. The front room was dimly lit and reeked of damp. It must have flooded frequently. The furniture was ramshackle and either a collection of eclectic leftovers from the seventies or a hipster's dream come true. Near the back of the room sat two mismatched armchairs of indeterminate colour. Spencer slumped into a mouldy chair and lit a cigarette.

"What's she done now?" His tone didn't indicate affection. Before they could answer, the old man picked up a can of bug repellent and sprayed a group of mosquitos in the corner of the room. "Damn buggers. They get in everywhere." There was no embarrassment— it appeared spraying bugs was as natural as smoking. He looked up, as if to say, *continue.*

Oleg's tone dripped of saccharine. "We wish to speak to her. We think she may be in danger and are trying to get a message to her. We thought you may be able to assist us."

Spencer took a drag and nodded to the two men standing before him. "And who are you lot then?"

"My name is Yeltsin." Oleg motioned to Bishop. "And this is my scrappy sidekick, Jeeves."

Bishop clenched his teeth and said nothing.

With a grunt, Spencer tapped ash into an ashtray. "You blokes are wasting your time, I'm afraid. Astrid is my daughter, yes, but I haven't heard from her in years."

Under normal circumstances, Bishop's heart would

have sunk, but he sensed there was more at play. Something about the whole set-up seemed off, but he couldn't put his finger on what.

Before Bishop could ask a question, Spencer went on. "You're not the first to turn up here looking for my Astrid, let me tell you. Nor will you be the last, I'm guessing. Although I have to say, you're more polite than most of the blighters, that's for sure."

"I dare say the others have had a different association with Astrid."

The old man nodded at Bishop as if he knew what he meant. "That right?" He squinted at each man in turn. "Did one of you gentlemen have a relationship with my daughter?"

At the same time, both Oleg and Bishop replied, "Yes."

The two men exchanged glances. Oleg glared, as if to say, *I'm in charge*. Bishop returned an expression that he hoped projected, *no, you're just a big git*.

With a polite cough, Oleg went on. "We have reason to believe Astrid may be in danger. We wish to speak with her about keeping out of harm's way."

"Right." The phone in Spencer's pocket vibrated. He took it out, read a message and smiled. The phone was the latest model Samsung; hardly in keeping with the man's decrepit surrounds.

"Keep her safe, that's lovely, good on you boys. Selfless, you are." Spencer took a drag of his cigarette and smiled. "I have a message from Astrid for you two."

"I thought you said—"

"She says she can't believe you'd be this stupid." Spencer's posh English accent disappeared, and was replaced with a Midwestern American one.

Oleg frowned. "How stupid?"

Bishop flung his hands in the air. "You had to ask."

Like lightning, Spencer drew a gun, far quicker than one would expect from such a weathered old man. It was more like a cowboy's quickdraw.

Spencer stood and flicked the Colt Defense pistol towards Oleg. "Alright, Ruskie, piece on the floor nice and slow, then kick it over here so I don't have to shoot your fucken' face off. There's a good boy." He snapped his fingers to emphasise the need for speed.

Oleg did as he was asked. The old man well and truly had the drop on them. He was well trained, kept out of striking distance, knew who was armed, and his unwavering gun hand didn't move. When Oleg had kicked the gun over, Spencer pointed with his gun, gesturing for them to sit on the armchairs either side of the coffee table.

"Make yourselves comfortable, boys. I'm expecting company any second, which will be nice for me, but fatal for you, I dare say." His maniacal laugh would have put any Disney villain to shame.

Turning to his companion, Bishop put on his best faux Russian accent and waggled his head from side to side. "Russian intelligence. Best in the world."

# CHAPTER FOUR

Not-Astrid's father paced about the room looking pleased with himself. Bishop didn't take him for an assassin, but looks could be deceiving. His demeanour had transformed completely. No longer the world-weary hunched old man, he now carried himself as if much younger. And far more arrogant.

For the third time in a minute, he checked the weathered window facing the lane. "I don't know what you boys have done, but you sure pissed off the wrong folks, let me tell you." He continued to pace. "Soon as I said you were here, they shot their wad."

He talked too much for an assassin. Far too much.

He went on. "The lady herself is going to be so pleased. When I talked to her, you could tell she had something nasty cooked up for you, all special like."

Oleg and Bishop exchanged glances. Did he mean he'd spoken to Astrid personally?

The mercenary must have realised he'd said too much. "But you ain't goin' nowhere." He raised his pistol to emphasise the point. "You might as well get comfortable."

"That's easy for you to say." Bishop was in full tactical mode, analysing every scenario, every response. "But it's hard to get comfortable with all these mosquitos about."

Oleg muttered harshly, "The man has a gun on you and you're talking about bugs?"

Bishop ignored him and spoke to their captor. "I'm being eaten alive here."

The old man again checked the window, then turned back and nodded his head. "Been stuck in this fucken room for days. Stinks, and the damn things never stop buzzing." A callous grin crossed his lips. "But it all paid off in the end."

"I'm sure." Bishop smiled amicably. "I'm deliriously happy for you, but in the meantime, do you mind if I..." He nodded to the can of bug spray. "I don't want to be scratching for the rest of my life. As brief as that may be."

The old man seemed to find the comment amusing, and nodded. Bishop bowed his head in thanks. Oleg glared at him with wide eyes, thinking he'd gone mad. Bishop ignored him and waited for the mercenary to check the window again. When he did, Bishop reached for the bug spray. That wasn't all he grabbed. Oleg saw the move and realised what was coming. He placed his hands on the arm of the chair, ready to propel himself forward when the moment came.

With the bug spray in his left hand, Bishop gave the can the briefest of taps. Their guard watched, but seemed unconcerned. When he checked the window again, Bishop sprang into action. Launching himself from the chair, he aimed the spray at his captor as he flung the man's lighter in front of it. The stream of fire was already on the man by the time he turned. Careening forward, Bishop thrust his impromptu flamethrower in the man's face.

Reeling backwards into the front door, the screaming

man's hands flailed against the fire engulfing his head. Bishop followed him, unrelenting, keeping the flame against the piteous man's blazing skull. The smell of burning flesh and hair was horrific, but Bishop kept the blowtorch on target. The man's thrashing body slumped against the door, the pistol falling to the floor as he desperately attempted to put out the agonising flames.

Oleg picked up the pistol and fired. The single bullet extinguished the man's pain. They picked up a rug and threw it over his head, doing the same to the flames. In the tiny confines of the room, the stench of charred flesh and hair was overwhelming. They paid it no heed. They couldn't afford to. They had bigger concerns.

Oleg handed the dead man's pistol to Bishop and extracted his own from Not-Astrid's father's scorched jacket.

"The way he was checking the window, I believe they will be here any second, da?"

Bishop looked back at the tiny, smoke-filled room. "This is not somewhere we want to be cornered."

"Agreed." Oleg gripped the front door handle. "On three." He inhaled deeply and spoke quickly. "Three." Without waiting, Oleg yanked the door open and sprinted into the lane.

Bishop sighed. "You big idiot."

In the laneway, Oleg aimed his gun towards the Grand Canal, then pivoted in the other direction and was blasted off his feet. The sound of the gunshot boomed across the narrow streetscape.

The big Russian was propelled backwards. He hit the ground hard with an agonised grunt and his gun clattered out of his hand. Bishop sprang into the laneway sideways and low to the ground, positioning himself between Oleg and their assailants. Firing the pistol in both hands, he took out the bearded man dressed in a tan business suit. He fell to his knees and collapsed with an extra hole in his chest.

The man's companion dove for cover. Bishop caught only the briefest of glimpses before she leapt from harm's way, but it was enough. The flash of long blonde hair gave it away. There was only one person it could be.

With his gun trained on where she had been, Bishop crawled to Oleg. He hadn't moved. The big Russian lay spread-eagle in the centre of the laneway.

Bishop scrambled to look at the Russian's face to see if he was conscious. Or alive. "Oleg!"

A big hand pushed Bishop's face away. "Very loud." He coughed and winced. Pulling down the collar of his shirt, he revealed a black garment beneath. "Bulletproof vest." He wheezed. "Latest Russian technology, very lightweight, very good." He sucked in a painful lungful of air and pushed Bishop gently. "Go. I'll catch up."

Bishop didn't need to be told twice. He sprinted towards where the assailants had been. Where Astrid had been. Bounding over the motionless body of the gunman —likely her bodyguard—Bishop ran.

In the meandering streets, his quarry could easily slip into an alcove and stage an ambush. He had to be careful, but if he was too cautious, he could let Astrid outrun him. Deciding haste was preferable to caution, Bishop tore after his prey.

Weaving through throngs of tourists, he raced into a small piazza. In the far corner he spotted a flash of blonde hair disappearing over a bridge and down another laneway. He was closing in.

Bounding after her, Bishop drew gasps from passers-by—tourists, shocked to see an armed man running on their leisurely saunter through historic Venice. If he lost Astrid in the labyrinth, he'd lose her forever. He couldn't let that happen. He *wouldn't* let that happen.

Sprinting over the bridge he heard a gondolier beneath singing an off-key rendition of 'You Must Remember This'. An experienced runner, Bishop performed deep belly breathing and kept a steady rhythm. Bounding over yet another humped bridge, he ran into the vast expanse of St. Mark's Square. Pigeons fluttered out of his way as he wove around tourists, trying to frame an Instagram-worthy shot or take the perfect selfie.

Near the entrance of Caffè Florian he saw a blonde figure doubled over, inhaling deeply. Bishop's stride didn't falter. He careened onward, his target set. The woman turned and searched the crowd. Her gaze fell on Bishop, now halfway across the square and closing in. Her mouth dropped open and she turned and ran. Bishop had seen her face. It was Astrid. He was close. So close.

The woman could move. Racing towards Museo Correr, Astrid disappeared under an archway. Bishop lost time arcing around a large group of school children, but soon sighted her once more. Dior and Chanel stores flashed by, then Astrid turned left into Campiello Traghetto, with Bishop close behind.

He turned down the narrow laneway and skidded to a halt. At the far end of the laneway, Astrid jogged into the entrance of the Gritti Palace Hotel. But that's not what made Bishop halt. It was the four musclebound men at the entrance with Uzis slung across their chests. The lane was long, with no place to hide or take cover. If he attempted a frontal assault with one gun and half a magazine, he'd be guaranteed a brutal and bloody death.

Strolling casually away, the MI6 agent kept the hotel in his peripheral vision. He knew where Astrid was. He needed to tactically assess the situation. Bishop needed to wait. His time would come.

~

Bishop sipped the sugary cocktail. It was offensive in both taste and price. From his vantage point at the table of the restaurant at the Hotel Alta, he was able to see any land-based exit from Astrid's hotel down the street. Water-based exits were covered as well.

"How're the ribs?" Bishop held the phone to his ear and spoke quietly.

"Still broken." The big Russian sounded pained. "Sitting in this rocking boat is doing wonders for them, let me tell you."

Oleg was positioned in a water taxi across from Gritti Palace Hotel, in case Astrid decided she needed a fast getaway. Of course she chose that particular hotel: five star, and two thousand dollars a night. Her faux-father's damp, mosquito-infested squalor wasn't exactly her style.

The sun was setting, casting a soft glow over the streets. Normally Bishop found Venice at sunset magical, but not tonight. The anger boiling in his belly made it impossible for him to appreciate the scene. He only had one thing on his mind.

"I have question for you, Bishop."

"I'd say shoot, but I'm afraid you'd take it literally."

"Why are you here?" Bishop started to answer but Oleg cut him off. "Yes, revenge blah blah. Reflex answer, fine. But that is not what I asked. I received a message from our source within MI6. You are missing, did you know this? You don't seem missing. So, I ask again, Charles Bishop, Englishman. *Why* are you here?"

It seemed the cat was out of the bag. MI6 were after him too. He'd add them to the list.

Bishop spoke quietly as he watched a group of four elderly tourists argue over a map. "You know how, when you see a 'wet paint' sign you can't help but touch it? Or you're at a bar and someone says 'don't look now', you look, right? That's Astrid."

"Bah!" Oleg made an annoyed grunt. "Nyet. That is stupid answer from stupid man. I think you are like the boy with finger in dyke."

Bishop blinked several times. "I have to see where this is going. Continue."

"You think you are the only one to plug the dyke."

"We have to work on your use of English idioms, Oleg."

"Like the little Dutch boy, only you can stop Astrid, regardless of danger and obstacles. Only the amazing fancypants Charles Bishop can do it."

Even though Oleg couldn't see him, Bishop shook his head. "That's not the meaning of the story."

"Well, what do you think it means?"

"It's an allegory. Meaning it's an attempt to stem the advance of something undesirable that threatens to overwhelm you." Bishop paused and snorted. "Maybe you're inadvertently right, Oleg. Because I fear Astrid, and because I'm oddly drawn to her, maybe I'm hunting her down to confront that fear. To overcome it. Perhaps I need to prove to myself that I'm more than a blunt instrument, that I can fear something, even be attracted to it, and still perform my duties perfectly."

There was a pause. "I think it is more the thing I said, Englishman."

"Do you have psychiatrists in the SVR, Oleg?"

"Da. Best in the world."

"Maybe this is more for them than the likes of us."

"For first time, I agree with you." Oleg paused. "What is situation?"

"No movement. Yet."

They continued to wait. They had to. A frontal assault on the hotel would be suicidal. Walking through the front entrance would be tantamount to barging into a lion's den wearing a meat suit. Even Oleg's suggestion of fake moustaches was unlikely to result in anything short of ending the night with a head like a colander.

"Englishman."

"Yes?"

"I should tell you something." Oleg paused. Bishop thought he heard hesitancy, something he'd never seen in the big man. "You saved my life in the lane. You did not need to do this."

"Look, Oleg, I appreciate what you—"

"Shut your stupid pretty face." Oleg went on, "You should know. I am not here to arrest Astrid. Not after what she has done to my country. She is responsible for the death of thousands with her illegal weapons. I know the two of you have this… thing, but you should know, if I have the chance… she has escaped justice so many times. If the chance arrives… I have to kill that woman. Do you understand?"

"We can have her arrested, extradited to the UK, I can—"

"I have orders, Bishop." Oleg's words were hard. "Do you understand what I am saying to you?"

Inhaling unsteadily, Bishop nodded slowly. "I understand, Oleg."

The Russian had kill orders from the SVR. That changed the dynamic significantly. The two were no longer a team; they were operating on different agendas. It only magnified the fact that Bishop, and Bishop alone, had to be the one to find Astrid.

The two spies waited in silence. They had been in position for over an hour and hadn't seen any sign of her. Bishop figured they would soon enough. Astrid saw him in St. Mark's Square. Her little trap had backfired. She'd certainly be chastising herself for underestimating him and undermanning the operation. In their short time together, she knew Bishop would not take the worldwide threat on his life lying down. Astrid would know the danger she was in. It was her move.

It came sooner than expected. Emerging from the entrance of the hotel, Astrid was protected by a large sunhat and four heavyset bodyguards. She looked stunning in a beige jumpsuit, striding down the laneway in heels. The bodyguards stuck to her like honey. That only made Bishop's mind wander to poured honey. On Astrid. It wasn't exactly helpful.

"She's on the move." Bishop slapped a wad of euros on the table. "Four bodyguards, covering her close. Heading north, towards my position. No visible weapons, but there's no way these guys aren't armed to the teeth."

"Four is too many, Bishop." Oleg sounded genuinely concerned.

"For you maybe."

"For anyone. Do not let your revenge cloud your view. There will be another opportunity to catch this woman. Do not—"

Bishop hung up. He didn't want Oleg's help, for many reasons. He had to do this and it had to be now.

Astrid's posse came closer, scanning the street. She looked panicked. The poor dear. Bishop walked diagonally away from them, ensuring he wouldn't be seen as a threat. He made his way towards the elderly tourists he'd been watching earlier. A fat man in a loud shirt unfolded a large map and shook it.

"I tell you, woman, we've already passed it!"

The two women tutted. Using the map as cover, Bishop sidled up close. A woman in a 'Rome' t-shirt looked at him oddly. Astrid's goons came closer.

When his prey were ten metres away, Bishop stepped forward. "You're all wrong. There it is!"

Bishop pointed at the centre of the map. With his gun. And fired. The tourists screamed and ran. The map fluttered to the ground. Astrid's lead bodyguard fell, the centre of his crisp white shirt turned crimson. The remaining three went for their shoulder holsters.

Bishop clipped the second with a headshot as he struggled to draw his gun. The third was mid-draw when Bishop plugged a bullet into his centre mass. He fell backwards, all expression slain from his face. The final goon, at Astrid's rear, made a terminal mistake. Believing it was an assassination, he pushed in front of his ward to shield her. But Bishop wasn't there to kill Astrid. Just the bodyguard. The moment he had a clear shot, Bishop took it. The goon's head snapped back and he fell onto a stunned Astrid. She gently shoved him away, letting him drop to the ground, lifeless.

Four rapid-fire shots. Four clean kills.

Astrid stood in the centre of the carnage, splattered with blood, but didn't scream. Others did that for her. Tourists ran in all directions, shrieking.

Gun trained on her, Bishop approached rapidly, eyes scanning the thinning crowd for more of Astrid's men. She stared at him, stunned.

Bishop never moved the gun from her. "Isn't it funny the people you run into when you're abroad?"

Astrid glared at him, wide-eyed. It wasn't shock, more surprise. In fact, she hardly seemed phased by the deaths at all. It's not every day four people die in quick succession right next to you, the surprise soon dissipated. Bishop watched her blood-splattered face closely. In a matter of seconds, it morphed. The transformation was remarkable. She went from surprised shocked victim to self-assured aristocrat in the blink of an eye. There was a reason the woman was formidable.

She raised an eyebrow. "I do hope you don't expect me to carry my own bags?"

Bishop stepped over the bodies and gripped Astrid's upper arm. Pulling her from the bodies, he shoved her away from the canal. "You won't need any luggage where we're going."

Her teeth shone, but there was no missing the fear in her eyes. "My, you are forward. Are we going on a date?"

"Something like that. We're off to the United Kingdom Consulate. I hear they do a Yorkshire pudding that's been referred to as barely edible."

"Sounds delightful." Astrid stopped and planted her fists on her hips. "Why don't you hand me over to the Italian police?"

"Oh sure, because there is absolutely no history of anyone bribing an Italian government official." Bishop grasped her arm and dragged her away from St. Mark's Square, where he knew there would be a high concentration of police. "No, it's the good old UK legal system for you, my dear. I'll call MI6 and they'll extradite your perfect arse to Old Blighty where you won't have a chance of bribing your way out."

"I'll give it a red hot go."

"I have no doubt." Bishop smiled. "And by then it won't be my problem."

They scuttled down the narrow streets of Venice. Bishop kept an iron grip on her arm and the gun tucked under his jacket but aimed at his quarry. Before long, the crowds grew thinner and less panicked. The news of the violent scene hadn't travelled this far yet. He knew the general direction of the Consulate, but wanted to be further away from the carnage before he stopped to gather his bearings.

"Very ballsy." Astrid smirked. "But I expect that from you."

Bishop ignored the quip. Deciding they'd covered enough ground, he pulled Astrid aside and pushed her against a wall.

She growled pleasurably. "Against the wall? You do know what I like."

His splayed palm kept her in place. "Stay."

"I'm not a dog." She shrugged. "Although I would be open to a collar. Just saying."

Bishop pulled out his phone and searched for the address of the consulate. He'd need to get a taxi and take the bridge off the island to the mainland. It was a hassle, but in twenty minutes he could hand Astrid over and it would be done.

The gun pointed at his temple said otherwise, however.

"I want you to give me the gun, nice and slow. I think you understand what will happen if you try anything." The accent was Italian. It was even, calm and, Bishop had to assume, professional.

The instant he'd felt the gun against his head, Bishop had assumed it was Oleg. It wasn't. So who the hell was this guy?

Bishop did as requested and presented the gun, holding the barrel. It was snatched away. Astrid pushed herself off the wall and turned to him. Her face didn't show relief. If anything, more fear had crept into her stunning blue eyes.

The gun to Bishop's head was held by an ugly hulking man in a leather jacket with a nose that had been broken more times than election promises. Beside him were two similarly clad and equally ugly henchmen.

Bishop tried to stand tall, but came up a foot short

beside the lead man. "Is this about those library fines again?"

Before anyone answered Bishop's question, a white hood was thrown over Astrid's head. Then Bishop's. Flex cuffs were pulled tight around his wrists. He heard the same being done to Astrid.

"Do you want us to kill him, ma'am?"

Bishop knew there was only one person they could be referring to. There wasn't much he could do to prevent his fate.

There was a pause. "Oh, you're talking to me?" Astrid's voice sounded as surprised as Bishop was. "Er, no. Not right now. But, ah, thank you for asking."

The two of them were manhandled and shoved forward for about fifty metres before being thrown in the boot of a car. The boot was slammed shut, and the sound of three car doors slamming soon followed.

In the trunk of the car Bishop twisted his hooded head to where Astrid lay. "Did you kidnap yourself?"

"This isn't my doing, Bishop."

"Who are these guys?"

"If they're not yours… absolutely no idea."

The engine started and through the hood Bishop could just make out the faintest illumination of the stop lights.

"Well then." Bishop sighed. "Won't this be fun."

# CHAPTER FIVE

The car went over a bump, followed by the rhythmic thrum of a highway. They must have been on the Liberty Bridge, heading away from Venice to the mainland. Bishop considered asking if they would be so kind as to drop them off at the UK consulate but thought it unlikely, even if he asked very politely.

Astrid pushed herself backwards, forcing Bishop to spoon her in the cramped confines of the car boot. "Cosy, isn't it?" Her voice was sultry.

"I've been in tighter places."

"I know, I remember." She ground her rear end into Bishop's crotch. "Every time I think of it, it gives me the warm tinglies."

"You have a problem, you know that?"

"You have no idea."

"I have a bit of an idea."

In the distance, the distinct sound of multiple police sirens made them pause. Both Bishop and Astrid held their breath. The sirens grew louder and louder until they were almost deafening, but then grew faint and steadily disappeared into the night.

"You ever see *Out of Sight*?"

"I… I don't… What?"

"The film *Out of Sight*. George Clooney, Jennifer Lopez? Sexy as hell. He just escaped prison, she's a US Marshal. They get locked in a boot together. They talk for a while and fall in love. Seriously underrated movie."

"Are you sure this isn't your doing, Astrid? Did you recreate a movie to try and force us together?"

"That would be nuts."

Bishop waited. "You didn't answer my question."

Astrid huffed. "No, I didn't orchestrate this. God. What do you take me for?"

Considering the circumstances, Bishop thought it best not to answer. "Fine. If it's not you, do you have any idea who these goons are?"

"None. It's not the police, obviously—throwing folks in trunks isn't usually their thing. A rival would have me in concrete boots at the bottom of the canal by now."

Bishop nodded to no one in the dark confines of the trunk. "But they were polite enough to ask if you wanted me dead."

"And yet you haven't thanked me for declining their offer."

Bishop ignored the comment. "So, who are they?"

"Trust me, I honestly don't know."

"Trust. Sure."

He highly suspected Astrid had spared his life because she wanted him close by if things got violent. It wasn't magnanimity. It was survival.

Astrid snuggled into Bishop and leant her head on his shoulder. "Oh, don't be like that. You know as well as I do that if we met under different circumstances, we'd hit it off, you and me. Like, if we met in a bar." She sighed. "I'm thinking a sophisticated old place—weathered, wood panelling, dark and cosy. Where you can get a decent whiskey sour or an old-fashioned. Dark, time-worn, cool as fuck. I'm at the bar alone and you come up to me, cocky as all get out, and ask if you can buy me a drink. No cheesy lines, no game playing. We both know what we want."

Under the hood, Bishop shook his head. "Is this how you fantasise it would be, Astrid? We're not those people. We never will be."

She nudged him with an elbow. "Admit it, Bishop, we have a connection."

"Then why do you keep trying to kill me? You could, you know, ask me out for a drink instead."

"Would you go?"

"No."

"And so here we are."

*She's deranged.* Bishop did his best to keep his temper in check. "You're saying all this, the bounty, everything, is because I wouldn't go on a date with you?"

"Not entirely, no."

"Well, what's the rest of it?"

"Honestly?"

"It's a good place to start."

Astrid ran her manacled hand down his arm. "It gets me off."

"I'm going to have to pause here for a moment. It what?"

Astrid gave a slight snigger. "It gets me off, Bishop. No matter what I throw at you, you come out on top. I know you love being on top." She ground herself into him again. "I don't know how you do it, but you survive, every time. I sent an entire *city* after your perfect arse and what did you do? Not only survive, you ended up getting the girl."

"Arresting the girl. Not that it did any good."

Bishop felt Astrid shrug. "A date or an assassin's bullet—either way, I take you out."

Bishop offered no reply.

Astrid nudged him. "Oh, come on, that was funny."

"This may come as a shock to you, Astrid, but having well-trained armed men trying to kill me is not high on my list of enjoyable pursuits. In fact, it's right up there with a root canal with no anaesthetic, or attending a six-year old's birthday party and offering my testicles up as a piñata."

Astrid scoffed. "Khalil Gibran said, 'Out of suffering have emerged the strongest souls; the most massive characters are seared with scars.' You keep surviving, Bishop, because we're fated, don't you see that? I told myself in Haiti after I put the bounty on your head, if he survives this, our destinies are intertwined. When you showed at the airport, I was so conflicted. You survived, but you still wanted to put me away. It was very confusing."

"I can see how it would be, all the way over in Crazyland."

Bishop was certain it wasn't an act. Astrid was deranged. No one in their right mind could ever conceive what she was saying was rational. They weren't fated. They weren't star-crossed lovers. The woman was completely certifiable.

If pressed, Bishop would admit he was attracted to Astrid, but that didn't come close to negating her unhinged view of the world. Perhaps Astrid was his punishment for his casual ease with women. Was this the universe paying him back for all the women he'd bedded so effortlessly? It was a good theory, except Bishop didn't believe in universal karma or predestination. Perhaps Astrid was here to prove him wrong.

Regardless of the reason Astrid had chosen Bishop as

the figure of her torment, he was still an MI6 agent at heart. He needed answers.

"Why go to all the trouble with the ship, the *Valkyrie*? That seems elaborate, even for you."

"Which part, the ship or bringing you into it?"

"Choose one."

"The ship was straightforward. Ports had begun refusing her, so she was end of life. I needed to get an urgent shipment of arms into Russia. Oslo was an obvious choice."

"And the photo of me?"

"Just some fun."

"The bullets aimed at my head say otherwise. Also, not necessarily the most fun for those gents whose brains I had to air out. If it wasn't for you, they would be alive and down the Neanderthal pub, grunting at one another and trying to figure out how wheels work."

"Like I said, it gets me off." Astrid's bound hands glided towards the front of Bishop's pants. "Maybe I could return the favour?"

Bishop slapped her hand away. "Terribly sorry to disappoint, but unlike you, death isn't an aphrodisiac for me. What about the crew? Why did they have to die?"

With an annoyed grunt, Astrid slumped backwards. "They threatened to contact Interpol unless I paid them double the already agreed, and rather generous, price. So it was a happy coincidence I needed to retire the ship and garner your attention."

"Not so happy for the crew, I would suggest."

The car went around a sharp turn, shunting them to the left. Both Astrid and Bishop paused until the vehicle continued on its way. was no stopping.

Astrid sighed heavily. "The Bishop I knew was far more fun than this."

"You never knew me, woman. This fantasy you've

built in your head isn't me. It's a twisted notion that isn't anchored to the real world at all."

"You're just playing hard to get."

"I..." Bishop closed his eyes—a redundant exercise with a hood over his head. "… need some sleep."

"But I want to talk. Who knows what stimulating things may pop up."

Bishop slapped Astrid's hands away once more. "We don't know where these men are taking us. It could be hours. We need to rest, to be ready when an opportunity presents itself. I'm going to sleep. I suggest you do the same."

"George Clooney wouldn't have gone to sleep if Jennifer Lopez was next to him."

"You're not Jennifer Lopez."

Huffing, Astrid rolled away. "If you're not going to play, I'll just have to entertain myself."

"Fine, please do it quietly."

"Oh, don't you remember, Bishop? You know me, I'm very… *very* vocal."

Bishop found it impossible to sleep.

The journey was indeed hours. Unable to see his watch, Bishop was unsure how long they'd travelled, but guessed around ten hours. If it was a simple murder, there surely would have been ample locations for them to be removed from the car and shot. They must be headed somewhere in particular. Given the starting point was Northern Italy, they could be anywhere in Italy, or indeed, Europe by now.

The car had slowed several times, but try as he might, Bishop found it impossible to detect any sound that would identify a particular country. It's not like French lorries had a particular accent or Austrian car horns had a distinctive inflection. He'd given up trying. Bishop had to be ready when an opportunity presented itself.

The car slowed and turned. The tyres crunched along a corrugated road. They'd left the roadway.

Nudging Astrid, Bishop did his best to shake his languid body awake. "I think we're here. Be ready."

Astrid twisted and curled her lithe body, making sure she caressed herself against Bishop in the process. "And what exactly are we going to be ready for? Clowns with scythes?"

"Why?" Bishop jolted up, bumping his head in the process. "Why would you say that? That's terrifying."

The boot flew open and several hands yanked him free. He heard movement that suggested the same was happening to Astrid. Heavy hands forcibly propelled Bishop forward, his legs unsteady from inactivity. Their collective footfalls sounded like they strode along a paved walkway. The light wind rustled foliage, and there was the subtle sound of flowing water in a fountain. In the distance Bishop could make out the splash and hum of a swimming pool. Wherever they were, it wasn't a quarry. *What the hell is going on?*

They were led up multiple flights of steps and pushed into seats. Bishop's flexicuffs were cut and his hood yanked off. The flood of bright sunlight blinded him, and it took several seconds before he was able to see anything. When his eyes adjusted, it wasn't what he expected. He and Astrid sat on a wide, luxurious terrace overlooking lush rolling hills, possibly part of the same estate. Before them was a grand table overflowing with fruits, breads, pasta dishes and bottles of wine. On the opposite side of the table sat only one person.

The woman sitting before them was in her mid-fifties, impeccably dressed in a white linen suit. Her face was quite handsome. It was plain to see she had been stunning in her youth. Age may have stripped the last vestiges of youthful vigour, but the shadow of her former beauty remained. She could still turn heads, Bishop was sure. Her jewellery was minimal but exceedingly expensive. She held herself with the air of someone who knew her exact place in the world. At first glance, Bishop surmised she was a dignified woman who tried to conceal her longing for her youthful splendour.

In the four corners of the terrace were guards armed with compact machine guns and earpieces. On the distant hills, similarly clad sentries patrolled. If the forced abduction wasn't clear enough, the guards completed the tableau. This was no casual chat.

The woman smiled broadly. "Welcome, my friends. Please," she motioned to the table, "you must be famished after your journey. May I recommend the linguine all'aragosta o all'astice; the linguine with lobster. My chef's specialty. Also, the tonnarelli with urchin eggs is to die for." She smiled, showing unnaturally white and straight teeth. "Not literally, obviously. You only just arrived."

Her manner was outwardly friendly, but Bishop detected a harshness, a menacing undercurrent she couldn't mask. This woman was clearly dangerous.

"What is this about?" Bishop asked. "Who are you?"

Their involuntary host seemed momentarily taken aback that Bishop had spoken, but the false smile remained in place. "Lunch first, then business. It's the Italian way."

So they were still in Italy. The distance travelled meant they could be anywhere, although Bishop suspected they were somewhere in particular.

Their host broke off a piece of bread and motioned to the food once more. "Mangiare, mangiare."

Bishop was famished, and dehydrated. He didn't need to be asked again. He loaded his plate and Astrid followed suit.

Between mouthfuls, Astrid turned to him and gave a confused shrug.

Lowering his voice, Bishop told her, "This is not what I was expecting."

"It's better than the homicidal clowns, at least."

"Stop bringing that up!"

After two plates of food and countless glasses of water, Bishop was sated. The food was easily the best Italian he'd ever had. Their host nibbled here and there, but seemed pleased with her compulsory guests' appetites. She clicked her fingers and a minor army of waiters appeared and cleared the table within a minute. One returned with a dusty wine bottle and three glasses. Their host poured three glasses of red and raised both her glass and her eyebrows.

"From my family's vineyard. A '93, which I think is our best year. A toast, to our future business together."

Bishop left his glass untouched. "I'm not sure who you think you're dealing with, but I can assure you, you are quite mistaken, I'm afraid."

Their host blinked at Bishop several times before pivoting her focus to Astrid. "I wish to know, can this man be trusted?" She tilted her head sideways. "If you wish for him to be... removed, all you need to do is say the word and he will be dealt with."

Astrid turned from Bishop to their host. There was a subtle shift in her demeanour as she pretended to contemplate Bishop's fate. Perhaps she wasn't pretending. Gradually, Astrid's expression grew more self-assured. In fact, Bishop detected the faintest of smirks. "Thank you, that won't be necessary, for now, Ms...?"

"You have failed to answer my most simple question.

Can this man be trusted?"

Astrid nodded. "I will personally vouch for this man."

Bishop had to wonder if Astrid had momentarily spared his life in case she needed his assistance, because she wanted to end his life on her terms, or for some other unfathomable reason. With Astrid it was always difficult to tell.

Their host seemed unconvinced, and eyed Bishop with a level of scepticism. "Very well." She smiled more genially. "My name is Giuliana Pugliese."

"And where exactly are we, Ms Pugliese?"

"Giuliana, please. You are at my estate in the lovely hills of Calabria."

Bishop did his best not to roll his eyes. *Of course.* Calabria. The 'Ndrangheta. The Calabrian mafia. Not as well-known as the Sicilian Mafia, in recent years the 'Ndrangheta had become the most powerful crime syndicate in Italy and therefore, the world. MI6 had been trying to infiltrate their secret organisation for some time. Powerful and dangerous, 'Ndrangheta represented around five per cent of Italy's GDP, something like fifty billion euros in untaxed revenue a year. Drugs, prostitution, human trafficking, extortion and, unsurprisingly, arms dealing. Of course they wanted to talk to Astrid. They shared many common goals.

It seemed Astrid had caught on as well. She shifted in her seat, sitting a little higher. "So, this kidnapping is a business meeting?"

Pugliese tutted. "Kidnapping is an ugly word. Let us call it proactive appointment arrangement, shall we? We have much to discuss. But first," she turned to Bishop, "we must determine this man's place in things, if he has one. My people had been following you for some time, Ms Spencer, preparing for an appropriate approach, when this man executed your bodyguards. And yet you spared his life. It is a most confounding arrangement, I must say."

"You have no idea."

Pugliese shot Bishop a glare of pure ice, its meaning crystal clear. *Speak out of turn again and you're dead.*

She went on. "On your request, we did not execute this man, but if you wish to change your mind at any time, the service is available to you."

"A most generous offer." Astrid tilted her head in thanks.

Pugliese rhythmically tapped her fingers on the table while staring at Bishop. "I conduct my business in an open manner, Ms Spencer, and as such I must be honest with you. I am somewhat at a loss as to the nature of this man. Is he a bodyguard of some description? He murdered your protection detail in broad daylight. What sort of bodyguard shoots other bodyguards?"

Bishop shrugged. "A bad one?"

A tiny grin creased the corners of Pugliese's mouth. "He is humorous—a buffoon perhaps, but an amusing one. I may end up glad my people didn't shoot him straight away."

"Thank you." Bishop smiled at his host.

"Don't misunderstand me, sir, my graciousness extends only as far as Ms Spencer's hospitality"

"Oh, I think he knows how to keep me happy." Astrid's hand glided over Bishop's thigh.

*Deranged.* The word echoed around Bishop's brain. After all they had spoken about in the boot of the car, their abduction, the veiled threats by a senior member of the Calabrian mafia, Astrid still found time to make overtly sexual intimations. The woman was deranged.

Bishop's mind was already elsewhere. No matter what it took, he had to gather as much intelligence on Pugliese's operation as possible. The criminal syndicate had operated for years without a senior member ever being indicted, let alone found guilty. Taking down someone of Pugliese's seemingly high stature would seriously put a dint in the 'Ndrangheta's illicit trade of misery and death. But first he had to survive.

Pugliese watched Astrid's wandering hand under the table. "Ah, I understand now." She paused and frowned. "I think. Very well. We all need our little... diversions. Fine, as long your... plaything does not distract you from conducting business." She slapped her hands together. "I have arranged quarters for you to freshen up. There is a clean set of clothes. Please take an hour to wash and refresh. I do apologise, but before I was aware of your impromptu visit I had invited several business rivals for dinner. I do hope you don't mind if we all share a table."

Bishop raised an eyebrow. "Business rivals?"

"Indeed. With a portfolio as diverse as mine, it is inevitable one would make commercial decisions which are, shall we say, unpopular in certain circles. I like to eliminate such misunderstandings as soon as I can. I do hope you don't mind." Pugliese rose, ending the conversation. "We'll meet for cocktails at sundown; we can discuss business then."

Without waiting for an answer, Pugliese walked away and down the stairs. Three heavyset bodyguards appeared to ensure their host's suggestion was followed. Bishop and Astrid stood, and were escorted from the terrace.

Bishop contemplated jumping a guard, but to what end? The guard next to him would cut him down, or the next one, or the one after that. No, Bishop had to bide his time and wait for the odds to even out. The risk was that they never would.

～

Astrid emerged from the bathroom drying her hair, her smooth skin wrapped in a towel. "I don't trust her."

Bishop did his best to avoid looking in Astrid's direction as she prowled across the excessively large 'guest' accommodation with the confidence of a panther. "Really? I always trust underworld kingpins who kidnap me at gunpoint. Is queenpin a thing?"

He received no answer.

The two had been shown to a guesthouse adjacent to the main manor. Formal clothes had been laid out on the bed, a tuxedo for Bishop, a cocktail dress for Astrid. Each outfit was their exact size.

Astrid had initially suggested they shower together, but Bishop politely refused, and then bluntly refused, when Astrid became more insistent. She finally traipsed to the bathroom with a pout, but made sure she left the door open. While she showered, the MI6 agent scoured the room for listening devices. He found none, but that didn't mean they weren't well hidden.

Astrid dried her hair. "Oh, please. I've had worse business introductions."

"Do you ever wonder what your life would have been like if you'd been an accountant, or owned a taco truck?"

"I know exactly what it would have been like." A thin smirk crossed her soft lips. "I would have hung myself from boredom long before now."

"This life will be the death of you, you know."

"Ah yes, but what a life."

Her cheeky wink was almost convincing, but Bishop wasn't swayed. There was something in her eyes, a tiny sliver of doubt coiled around her expression. Did she regret her life? Did she wonder what it would have been like in the 'real' world? Was that why she pursued Bishop so relentlessly? Did she see him as a way of ending it all, one way or another? With an internal groan Bishop did his best to dismiss the thought. Freud would have referred to that particular line of thinking as transference. He didn't need to save Astrid, nor did he have to feed her fantasies. All he had to do was bring her to justice. was the sole thing he required from her.

"You could always join me in this life, you know?" Astrid's expression was good-humoured with a hint of hopefulness. "You're a drone for a government that's only ever looking out for the men in charge. You're not your own man, Bishop, don't you see that? You're in a cage."

Bishop shrugged. "It's a guest house apparently."

Astrid frowned. "No, your mind. You think you're on the good guy's side. There's no such thing. Good. Bad. It's all perception. You just have to let go of your ingrained dogma. Question your reality, Bishop. You've been brainwashed, you just won't admit it. If you want true freedom, I have it in spades."

It almost seemed like she was serious. He always found it hard to know with Astrid. In another reality he could see how another Bishop would be tempted. A life with no restrictions, no rules and unlimited potential. It was alluring. But Bishop didn't live in that universe. He had to concentrate on this one.

From the way she flitted about the guesthouse, Bishop never would have believed Astrid was a prisoner. She moved around the space as if preparing for a night on the town, seemingly without a care in the world. Perhaps she was so used to danger, so accustomed to the imminent threat to her wellbeing, that being held captive by one of the most brutal crime syndicates on the planet was hardly cause for concern. For all Bishop knew it could have been a weekly event. If so, he decided it would be rather difficult to make dinner plans.

With her back to Bishop, Astrid lifted the dress and let

out a low whistle. "Dior. The woman knows cocktail dresses. I might just move in."

Without warning she undid her towel and it dropped to the floor. The cello sweep of Astrid's back and her shapely behind stood before him. Her naked body was, without hyperbole, flawless.

As much as it pained him, Bishop looked away. "I wish you wouldn't."

"What? Wear a dress?" She flung it on the bed and turned to face him. Hand on hip, she presented an alluring figure. "My, whatever shall we do instead?"

Intently gazing at the paintwork on the ceiling, Bishop did his best to ignore temptation. Normally one to embrace such an appealing distraction, he forced himself to refocus. He waited until he heard the sound of a zip.

He looked down to see Astrid with the dress in one hand, still stunningly naked. "Zip works." The wickedness of her grin would have made Cruella de Vil blush.

"Well played." He turned to check if the paintwork on the wall was as well applied as on the ceiling.

"Oh, you should know how well I like to play."

Bishop went and had a cold shower. On his return, he concentrated on dressing himself. It was as if the suit were tailored for him. The Italians knew suits. He turned to Astrid, who was no longer naked. The effect was only slightly better. The black dress not only hugged her every curve, it enhanced each one, too. Bishop wondered if he had time for another cold shower.

Deciding to change the subject, he asked, "What's your impression of our host?" As he said the words he cupped his ear with his hand and pointed to all corners of the room. The message was clear: *the walls could have ears.*

Astrid scoffed. "Oh, please. If they have microphones, they'll have pinhole cameras." She sashayed forward and rubbed her slinky black outfit against his thigh. "If they're watching, how about we give them something interesting to watch? I like it when people watch."

"You're a walking book of psychological disorders, aren't you?"

Astrid let out a frustrated sigh. "And you're a prude."

Bishop baulked. "I can honestly say that's the first time anyone has ever accused me of that."

Giving a shake of her head, Astrid pushed herself away from Bishop to take in his outfit. "This is a great suit." She ran her fingers down the lapel. "Hard to know if I love you more in a suit or in nothing at all." The wickedness returned. "That was a silly thing to say."

The pounding at the door put paid to Astrid's wayward suggestions.

A gruff voice came from the other side of the door. "I am here to escort you to dinner." The tone seemed to indicate that the owner of the disembodied voice was unhappy with his role as escort.

Bishop motioned to the door in a gentlemanly manner and kept his tone low. "Be ready for anything."

His companion groaned. "Anything? That's absurd. I mean, what if she has mind-reading monkeys, or scythe-wielding clowns."

"You… you had to go there, didn't you?"

She poked him in the chest. "I like to know your buttons."

The two followed the shaved gorilla in a dinner suit to the main house, where they were led through a labyrinth of interconnecting rooms and stately halls. Every corridor had an armed guard. The security force was formidable, and impossible for one man to take on alone. Who was Bishop kidding? An SAS regiment would have a tough time with this lot.

They were led to a grand dining room. At its centre, a

ridiculously long and imposing dining table was laid out with elaborate centrepieces of flowers, baubles, candles and napkins contorted into a cacophony of zoological shapes. On either side of the two unoccupied seats sat what Bishop assumed were the rivals Pugliese had mentioned.

Astrid gasped.

None of the business rivals spoke. Not that Bishop expected them to. It would be rather difficult to speak when your head had been violently removed from your body, placed on a spike and positioned before an elegant dinner setting. The four heads sat on spikes, dripping blood; fresh kills.

At the head of the table sat Pugliese. The stately crime lord wore what could only be described as a cross between an elegant dinner gown and a roadkill peacock. She was clearly unconcerned at being surrounded by severed heads, and didn't seem to notice their approach. She was hunched over a mobile phone, tapping away at it with some frustration. It appeared to Bishop that she was trying to put in an access code. She grunted and picked up another phone from the pile beside her and began the process again. As Astrid and Bishop hesitantly made their way across the grand room, their host finally noticed them. She grinned and motioned for them to sit at the two vacant place settings in the middle of the table.

Bishop couldn't keep his eyes off the heads. It was a sick and twisted display, meant to intimidate and horrify. And as much as Bishop hated to admit it, it worked.

Bishop turned to Pugliese. Their host smiled amiably and raised her glass in salute. Her genial smile was a shallow veneer masking the vilest and most callous of minds. Pugliese continued to grin with a thoroughly victorious expression. The meaning was clear enough: *You will never leave this place alive.*

# CHAPTER SIX

Bishop had to force Astrid into her seat. She was rattled. And rightly so. Pugliese was certifiably unhinged. It was an unsettling day indeed when Astrid was only the second most deranged person in the room. Bishop wondered if he should have been issued a straitjacket instead of a dinner one.

Bishop did his best to return his host's soulless smile. "You certainly have a flair for a dramatic table setting. Tell me, are they chrysanthemums? I would have thought they were out of season."

Pugliese squinted. "My, you are a cool one, aren't you?" With a tilt of her head she creased her face in amusement. "First you take out an entire security detail without a scratch, then you don't flap an eyelid at the sight of a decapitated head. Who are you?"

Bishop shrugged. "In my defence, the chrysanthemums are most striking."

Pugliese let out a chuckle. "I'm not sure if you're dangerous, fearless or completely stupid."

"Can't I be all three?"

She narrowed her eyes. "What's your name, English man?"

"Joseph McGurkensquiter. My friends call me Joe."

A frown formed in the corners of her mouth. "Ah, now you're far less charming. You seem to have failed to recognise that my question was neither polite nor social." Her voice took on a razor-sharp tone. "Who are you?"

"No threat to your good self, I assure you."

Nodding, Pugliese reached out her hand and placed it atop the head of the rival to her left. "I heard those exact words just recently." Her fingers rhythmically tapped the skull. "So you will forgive me if I'm somewhat dubious as to the veracity of your claims." Her lips grew thin. "I still don't know if I trust you."

"You wished to talk about business?" Astrid seemed to have shaken off her initial shock and had once again generated the calm façade of a woman in control. Her voice smooth and calm, she went on. "I vouch for this man, I'd trust him with my life." She cast Bishop a sideways grin. "Anything you wish to say to me can be said in front of him. I'm sure you understand, I have much urgent business to attend to, but obviously not to the detriment to discussing a future partnership with you. I'm keen to understand the nature of your proposal."

The three sat in silence for some time. Their host steepled her fingers in contemplation, eying each of them in turn. Pugliese had positioned the rivals so that whenever Bishop or Astrid addressed her, they would always have a severed head interrupting the view.

Before anyone could speak, several waiters appeared carrying silver trays laden with appetisers. Thankfully the detached heads of Pugliese's foes didn't receive a serve. They obviously didn't have the stomach for it.

Amusement danced across her lips as Pugliese's gaze darted from Bishop to the bloody head next to him. "An unfortunate turn of events, I'm afraid." She sighed deeply. "I had invited these gentlemen here in good faith. For decades our families have been unnecessary adversaries, fighting needlessly when we should have combined our resources to combat the common enemy."

Bishop casually placed some bruschetta on his plate. "Clowns?"

Pugliese frowned. "The government."

Bishop held up a finger of understanding. "Ah."

She went on. "A government determined to interrupt our business dealings. We meet people's needs by supplying what they want, offering goods and services to those who have a desire that must be met."

"How magnanimous of you."

"Quite. I'm glad you understand. We generate a hefty portion of the economy, yet the authorities wish to quash our dealings in the most forceful and violent of ways."

*All the while you don't pay taxes, bribing or murdering officials to further your illicit trade.* Bishop thought it prudent to not mention this aloud.

"Thus, I invited Mr Salvo here," she reached out and tapped the head of the man to her left, "to see if we could come to some mutually beneficial accord. A détente, if you will. But I was betrayed." Her expression became dark, her voice took on a deep tone. "Salvo and his people came armed, despite my assurances that this was not necessary. He placed snipers at the edge of my property. In town he amassed a posse, armed to storm my compound during the night. And worst of all, he wished to take advantage of my generous spirit after I had expressly given my word. I'm sure you understand that such impertinence could not go... unpunished." She slapped her hands together and turned to Astrid. "But enough of that. As you seem so eager to discuss business, let's, as the Americans like to say, get down to it."

"Before we begin," Astrid's tone was self-assured, "I request a clarification." There was no waver in her voice, no tenor to indicate even an ounce of trepidation.

"Of course. Clarity is important in all one's dealings." Pugliese nodded as if to say, *proceed*.

"Our… journey to your lovely home, the display of your rivals' abject failure… one could, if one was of a cynical nature, construe these affectations as a form of coercion. I just wanted to be clear." Astrid smiled sweetly. "Your intimidation means shit to me. You want something from me, fine, let's talk, but your bullshit bullying tactics amount to nine tenths of fuck-all. You want clarity? Here it is. If I want to do business with you I will. If not, I'll tell you to shove it up your aristocratic Italian arse, no matter how many severed heads you plant around the dinner table. I haven't made it this far in my business by kowtowing to intimidation and threats." Astrid smiled a menacing smile, not altogether dissimilar to their host's. "Like I said, clarity."

Pugliese's stony demeanour didn't shift. "I've killed men for less impertinence."

Astrid folded her arms. "So have I."

The two women stared at each other for a full minute. It was Pugliese who broke first. A slow, seemingly genuine, grin crossed her face.

"Now I see the woman I have heard so much about. Now I understand why there are those who cower at the mere mention of Kali."

"Good." Astrid picked up her wine glass. "Now, what is it you want to discuss? You want a cut of my arms business?"

"No." Pugliese placed both palms down on the table. Bishop half suspected she was about to say, *I want all of your arms business*. Their host shook her head. "At least, not yet. We may discuss how I may assist *your* operations, but only after you and I know we can trust one another in our business dealings. Although I do appreciate your openness. No, my dear, I wish to discuss one item first. It concerns family. Well, doesn't everything? You see, I have something to offer you, and in exchange, I... I was about to say expect, but that is the wrong word. In exchange for this information, I *hope* you and I can become allies."

Astrid nodded at her. "I am your captive audience."

Their host ignored the obvious dig. "My dearest brother, Dario, the head of the 'Ndrangheta, is currently en route to Istanbul."

Bishop's struggled to keep his shock from showing. It surely couldn't be a coincidence that before Astrid's less-than-subtle interference in Norway he was prepping for an MI6 mission to Istanbul. Was all this somehow tied to that mission? *What the hell is really going on?*

Astrid sat up. "Perhaps we could discuss this," her eyes darted to Bishop, "at another time?"

Pugliese regarded both Astrid and Bishop. "Where you not the one who stated unequivocally that I could trust this man?"

"Yes, but..." Astrid shifted in her seat, doing her best to avoid eye contact with Bishop. "There are some business dealings which are, ah, more sensitive than others."

Pugliese leaned forward, beaming like a lioness watching a young zebra stray from the herd. "I believe your exact words were 'I'd trust him with my life'. You also assured me that anything could be said in front of him, and you personally vouched for him. Is that correct, or did I mishear?"

The challenge had been laid down. It seemed Astrid had backed herself into a corner. Bishop would have to stay or she would lose face. Perhaps literally. Bishop glared at Astrid. *What are you trying to hide from me, woman?*

The mention of Istanbul couldn't be coincidental. Bishop didn't believe in coincidences. The fact that he'd been pulled from an MI6 operation in Turkey meant there were larger cogs turning. Deep in his guts, Bishop sensed the worst. Nothing about the last few hours made much sense, but he had the gnawing feeling it soon would, and he was absolutely certain he wouldn't like it when it did.

In the absence of any further protests from Astrid, their host continued. "I understand through a trusted source that you, my dear, are the reason my beloved brother is venturing to the former Byzantium capital."

Astrid's back grew straighter. "I've never had dealings with your—"

Pugliese waggled a finger. "My apologies, poor choice of words. It is in response to your actions that my brother is personally making his way to Istanbul." She paused. "It seems Dario has found you are in possession of one Yousef Sharif, and wishes to kidnap the kidnapped for his own purposes. Or is the term 'rekidnap'? Either way, he's after the man currently in your possession."

It took every ounce of Bishop's training to not leap up, scream blue murder and throw anything he could get his hands on, humans included. Yousef *goddamn* Sharif. The man Bishop had been tasked with finding. The man who could disrupt the state of the world's economy. *That* Yousef Sharif. It was Astrid all along. Even before Norway their destinies had once again been intertwined. It was all linked, everything.

Oblivious to Bishop's inner turmoil, Pugliese went on. "Since learning of this kidnapping, one thing has had me perplexed. I know the OPEC vote is coming up on whether to increase the price of oil. I can only assume your... intervention has something to do with that. Tell me, was your intention to increase or decrease the price?"

Astrid glared back at Pugliese. "If what you say is

true and I am trying to manipulate economies, what good would come of shouting that particular secret?"

Letting forth a raucous laugh, Pugliese nodded. "A salient point. Quite ridiculous of me to ask, of course."

Lips pursed, Astrid frowned. "You seem… very well informed."

Pugliese frowned. "Do you plan to kill him?"

Astrid glanced sideways, but didn't make eye contact with Bishop. "No. If I did, he wouldn't be alive for your brother to try and take from me. I don't plan on irritating the Saudis if I can avoid it."

Pugliese nodded as if she knew what that meant. "The move from selling weapons to world extortion was quite the leap, I must say, but I do love a woman who ruthlessly pays no heed to the small-minded constraints of others. However, there is one question I must have an answer to." She slowly turned her gaze to the closest head on a spike. "How exactly will you ensure Sharif's compliance? He is a man of influence on the OPEC board, so can sway the vote, I am certain, but how does one kidnap a man and ensure his ongoing compliance?"

Her pointed glance to the severed head carried a clear meaning: *this question is non-negotiable*. Astrid's twisted lips told Bishop she knew it too, and was weighing up her answer.

"Sharif has certain… tastes that are not particularly in line with publicly held Saudi beliefs. I ensured that His Highness had ample supply of such men during his enforced sabbatical. He'll soon bed one of them and we'll have footage of these activities to remind him who his friends are. He'll be released in time for the vote, unharmed."

Pugliese shook her head in admiration. "The audacity is amazing. You are a formidable woman, I must say. I will take great pleasure in doing business with you, I am sure."

Under the table, Bishop gripped the sides of the chair to keep from throttling anyone. If this were a sanctioned MI6 operation Bishop would have pulled the pin then and there, and ensured that everyone within a hundred-metre radius was summarily renditioned and interrogated in some far-flung sand-infested hellhole. But this wasn't an MI6 mission. It wasn't remotely a mission of any kind. He was unarmed in hostile territory with no communications, backup or escape plan. What he wouldn't give for a phone, a knife and a machine gun right about now. And perhaps some Royal Marine Commandos.

Indifferent to Bishop's internal discord, Astrid went on. "Why would you tell me your brother was on the way to Istanbul?"

Pugliese sighed. "It is unfortunate to have to say, but I have become estranged from my family, my beloved brothers. They have excluded me from recent dealings after I, ah, forcefully but respectfully requested a bigger say in the organisation's strategic decisions. It was, shall we say, not gratefully received." She once again thrummed her fingers on the severed head beside her. "I believe they supported my rivals here, and encouraged them to take me out while my brother was out of town, as it were. So, you see, they have given me no option but to do what my family have been doing for centuries. We do not ask for respect, we grasp it with two bloody hands."

"You want me to kill your brother for you? So this is about revenge?"

"No, Spencer, this is not revenge. This is retribution. Do you know the origin of the word? It's an old French word derived directly from the Latin *retributionem*. The original meaning was evil given for evil done. Basically, divine punishment." Her smile was pure malice. "So, this is very much about retribution."

Astrid frowned. "You want me to enter into a family squabble?"

With a shake of her head, Pugliese's appearance took on a dark hue. "No. I wish you to end it. When my people identified your presence in Italy I acted, admittedly rashly, to deliver a simple business proposal to you. Believe me when I say our meeting will be most beneficial for you. This information is completely free, a taste of the benefits you will experience in our ongoing partnership. If we become business partners I will extend to you my network, contacts, boundless resources. Our agreement would save you having to deal with meddlesome middle men—we can handle all logistics with our global network. It is completely up to you, my dear." She smiled without humour. "But first I offer you this for free—a sampler, as the Americans call it. I simply wish to warn you, Astrid Spencer. I wish to ensure your ongoing success, that is all."

In spite of his internal furore, Bishop understood what Pugliese was really saying. Kill my brother or you're dead. Give me the inside running on how Sharif will influence OPEC or you're dead. Give me a huge cut of your arms business or you're dead. Basically, agree to my deal or you're dead. It was anything but a mere business transaction. Pugliese was not only proposing a hostile takeover of the 'Ndrangheta, she was exponentially expanding their already extensive reach. With an inside track on global oil prices and a stake in the biggest illegal arms dealing network in the world, she'd be all powerful. Drugs, prostitution, weapons were all just a means to an end for the mafia. All that meant was money. This was different. This meant power. Pugliese would become one of the most powerful people on the planet. It was audacious in its scope.

Astrid was actively avoiding eye contact with Bishop. She must have known that if it wasn't for their host he'd be wringing her neck. Astrid had somehow learned he was on the mission to Turkey and unleashed the assassins to remove him from the chess board. She'd left false clues to lead him to Venice and a likely capture. And now she'd lost control of the situation.

"What's in it for me?" Astrid folded her arms. "How do I know the 'Ndrangheta will help me?"

"Oh, but we already have, my dear. You don't believe your escape from the Haitian authorities was entirely your doing, do you? We have people everywhere. Didn't you wonder how I knew of your little sting operation in Venice? Which of your people suggested the location in Italy? Might his name be Julio?"

Astrid considered her words carefully. "He originally said Rome, but I preferred Venice."

"Yes, Rome was my favoured city, being somewhat closer, but Venice was a nice little compromise."

Astrid's jaw hardened. "That little…"

"It took us years to place him in your organisation. Julio is how my brother knows exactly where you're holding Sharif. My, it was quite the Herculean effort to even *find* your organisation. And now Julio has retired comfortably and never has to work again. We look after our own, Ms Spencer. As you will find out."

With a sigh, Astrid pushed her plate away, seemingly having lost her appetite. "Why do you want a cut of my business? You already deal in weapons."

"We do, yes, this is fact. However, selling a fourth-hand sawn-off shotgun to an inept Albanian bank robber is not the same as selling an entire weapons array to a rebel Pakistani faction, I am sure you would agree?" She smoothed her linen suit. "I'm sure we can come to some mutually beneficial arrangement. We have a vast network at your disposal; it will certainly cut down overheads for you. And as for Yousef Sharif, you see how I am saving your life by giving up my own beloved brother. You see how I trust you implicitly already? We will do great things together, you and me. But, as I said, it is completely up to you, Ms Spencer." Pugliese patted the head beside her and gently brushed the hair away from his face. She turned to Astrid, her features as dark as the centre of a black hole. "Just agree or I'll hand you over to the Russian SVR, who I understand have no love for you." She broke into a raucous laugh. It was pure affectation. It was utterly bereft of humour. "I am kidding, of course. The choice is yours." She stood. "Now if you'll excuse me for a moment, I must determine the status of the efforts to round up my enemies in the town. Please enjoy your appetisers, I will be back for the pasta course." She issued an insincere smile. "So Italian. I'm such a cliché, I know."

She left without another word, leaving the two of them alone with their thoughts, and the severed heads. Bishop was too angry to even look in Astrid's direction. The icy silence was interrupted by a troop of waiters laying out the next course. While they arranged the arancini, bruschetta, cheese croquettes and antipasto, Bishop wondered if he'd have time to leap up and strangle Astrid before they could fight him off. He was weighing up the odds when Astrid leaned over and whispered to him, "I can explain."

Stabbing at an arancini ball with a fork, Bishop ignored her.

"The woman is obviously deranged." Eying the head next to her, Astrid continued. "I think we need to focus on what happens next."

Bishop flexed his hands. "I was just thinking about that."

"You mean escape?"

Bishop glanced at her neck. "Something like that."

"You mad at me?" From the corner of his eye, Bishop could see enough of Astrid's face to know she was pouting.

He put down his fork. "You orchestrated all of this. You put a price on my head. Took me off the mission to Turkey. Everything. This is all you. You wanted me out of the equation one way or another."

"No, you silly man, I protected you."

"You sent hired assassins to kill me. That's not traditionally what one associates with a feeling of safety. You could have warned me."

"Would you have listened?"

He was silent. They both knew the answer. There was so much more to the story than Bishop currently knew, and he was certain it would be far more twisted than Astrid was letting on. It always was with her.

With folded arms, Bishop scowled at Astrid. Her angelic face hid the evil within. "If you agree to her terms, Dario Pugliese will be walking into a trap. I can't say the world will miss the mob boss. But so are my team. They don't know they're heading into an ambush. Your people know my people are coming. They're dead but they don't know it yet. Don't expect me to thank you for that."

Astrid threw her arms in the air. "I saved *your* life. I can't protect all of MI6, Bishop. That's not my job."

"No." His face hardened. "It's mine."

Bishop stood and walked around to the pile of mobile phones Pugliese had been so interested in when they'd first arrived.

"What... what are you doing? You've seen the security the woman has. She's got mean-looking guards everywhere. Even you can't fight her singlehandedly."

"Who said anything about singlehandedly?" Bishop raised an eyebrow. "I'm going to need an army."

Bishop stood before the pile of phones Pugliese had been trying to unlock when they'd walked in. He picked up the most recent model and contemplated it for a moment.

Astrid watched him closely. "If we had the rest of their bodies we could try the fingerprint unlock."

Bishop nodded, only half listening. "I wonder…"

He strode to the head to the left of their host's chair, the leader called Salvo. Bishop pressed the unlock key and held the screen in front of the severed head. A second later the facial recognition software pinged.

Showing Astrid the unlocked screen, Bishop winked. "It's part of a spy's role to be adaptable."

"You totally fluked that!"

Bishop smirked. "I really didn't expect it to work."

Navigating to the call history, Bishop pressed the number that had most recently been called. It rang twice before being answered.

"Pronto."

Bishop spoke evenly. "Do you speak English?"

"Who is this?"

"Let's say I'm someone who has the same goals as yourself."

"Where is Salvo?"

"Are you a member of his organisation?" On receiving no answer, Bishop pressed on. "He called you as he would have been arriving at Pugliese's, so I'm guessing you are."

"Perhaps. What are you—"

Bishop interrupted. He didn't have time to waste.

"I'm sorry to inform you that was the last call he ever made."

"What... that witch!" Bishop heard distressed noises. "Why..." the man at the other end of the phone choked back tears. "Why should I believe you?"

Bishop took a photo of the disembodied head before him, then pressed send. "I just sent you all the proof you need that Pugliese has no honour."

The wailing at the other end told Bishop the message had been received all too clearly. "Dio cane! Andare a puttane! Cazzo Madre di Dio! Dare un calcio nel culo a qualcuno!"

"Listen." Bishop raised his voice. "Listen! I don't have much time. If you want revenge you need to act now. Pugliese is weak, that's why she killed Salvo—because he knew it. She thinks she's won, she's complacent. If you want to avenge your leader you need to attack now."

There was an icy silence. Bishop thought he may have overplayed his hand. The voice on the phone took on a sudden cold edge. "He was not just my leader, he was also my father. The dragon will pay for what she has done, be assured of that, friend."

The line went dead. Bishop returned the phone to the stack and took his seat.

Astrid leaned over, her face contorted in disgust. "You lied to those men. Pugliese isn't weak. You're sending them to their deaths."

Bishop shrugged. "They're all mafia. Murder, corruption, human trafficking—none of these people are innocent, they all have blood on their hands. There are greater things at play here. If I wanted—"

Bishop stopped as Pugliese re-entered the room. Nobody spoke. After crossing the vast room she flopped into her seat at the end of the table. Her mood seemed heavier than when she'd left. Remaining silent, she stared at the phones beside her and frowned. Did she realise she'd absentmindedly left her prisoners with mobile phones? Did she suspect what they had been up to? She turned from the phones and looked blankly at the table, as if her mind was elsewhere. Bishop eyed a carving knife at the centre of the table, just in case.

Her demeanour had definitely soured since she'd left, apparent confirmation she'd been unsuccessful in finding Salvo's men. If she'd only asked Bishop.

She didn't ask Bishop.

For ten minutes they poked at their food emotionlessly. Eventually Pugliese rang a small bell, drawing an army of servants who came and cleared the table. She remained mute, her elegant face showing visible signs of annoyance. Only when the table had been laden with bowls of steaming pasta did she speak.

"My apologies, I have been the most ungracious of hosts. You have caught me on such an irregular day. I normally have…"

Pugliese faltered as she reacted to a distant din. Bishop heard it too. It could have been a plate dropped. Just as easily, it might have been a gunshot.

Their host continued. "Excuse me. As I was saying, I normally—"

This time the noise was louder, and distinctly gunfire, coming from multiple sources. She stood, not knowing which direction to look. More to herself than anyone else, she said, "What… what is that?"

Bishop watched Astrid. She was wound like a spring, ready. She gave him the slightest of nods.

"Sounds to me," he turned to their host, "like retribution."

Bishop lunged for the knife as the first explosion lit up the windows.

# CHAPTER SEVEN

Pugliese turned but it was too late, Bishop had already leapt into action. By the time her eyes locked on Bishop, the carving knife was at her throat.

"Call out, please." He leant in close. "I'd love to place your head on a pike. I hear it's the in thing."

Pugliese sighed. There was no panic in her eyes. This was not the first threat to her life. "I believe your name is not really McGurkensquiter."

"You might be right about that." Bishop pushed her towards the nearest exit. "Get us to your car and you might even live long enough for me to give you a hint as to what it really is."

But it seemed fate couldn't wait that long. A door burst open and a distraught guard staggered through the nearest door.

He managed to splutter "Nemico" before skidding to a halt as he caught sight of Bishop holding a knife to his boss's throat.

Without waiting a heartbeat longer, Bishop flung the knife at the man, stabbing him deep in the Adam's apple.

As blood spurted from the wound, Bishop pushed Pugliese away and dove for the man, whose hands were clutching the bloodied knife. Ignoring the man's pitiful gurgled cries, Bishop tore the Uzi from his shoulder as two more guards lurched into the grand dining room on the far side.

Bishop foresaw the next few seconds clearly. It was a talent he'd always had; visualise every move, every foot-fall, every thrust, every parry. He didn't need to fight the entire compound. Just this room. Maybe the next. Perhaps the one after that. Eventually he would run out of either foes or luck. Regardless, it would end.

The guards hesitated, and hadn't yet pulled their triggers. Whether they were too afraid to hit their mistress or were still in shock, it didn't matter; Bishop had the drop. Firing evenly and at centre mass, he took down the first before the other managed to get into a firing position. When he did, his shots were hurried and way off target. He was clearly unused to firing under pressure—shooting ranges generally don't shoot back. Bishop took the second guard down with equal precision. As the two guards collapsed, Bishop swung the weapon at Pugliese. She stood next to Astrid and raised her hands with a nod at Bishop's ruthless efficiency.

Astrid stared at him wide-eyed, with the most wicked grin on her red lips. "I'm so wet right now."

Bishop grunted. He didn't have time for that, although he did allow himself a split second's diversion. Intending to strip the last two guards of their weapons, he tossed the Uzi to Astrid.

Except he never made it that far. Moving far faster than Bishop would have thought possible, Pugliese darted around Astrid and shot her arm out, grabbing the Uzi in mid-flight. She smashed Astrid in the chest with the butt of the compact machine gun, sending her staggering backwards. Now the only one armed in the room, a malevolent leer crossed Pugliese's lips.

*Stupid, stupid, stupid.*

He knew better. He *was* better than that.

There was something about Astrid that always put him off his game. Now he would pay for that distraction with his life. Astrid lay crumpled on the floor, wheezing from the blow.

"How dare you!" Pugliese stormed towards Bishop, who was standing over the first slain guard. "How dare you come into *my* home and kill *my* men! You will pay dearly for your impertinence."

Bishop bowed deeply, as if seeking absolution from the mafia boss. He was seeking no such thing.

Pugliese pushed the barrel of the gun in his face. Still in deep bow, Bishop's hand reached down and back, out of the line of sight of his captor. His fingers wrapped around the hilt of the knife still embedded in the guard's throat. In one swift move, Bishop rose, using his right forearm to deflect the Uzi as his left hand slashed the knife diagonally across Pugliese's face.

The woman's scream was guttural. She dropped the weapon as her fingers desperately clutched the two now-separated parts of her once-handsome face. As she collapsed, Astrid rose to her feet. Bishop clicked his fingers and pointed at the other guards' weapons. She expertly checked the clips, then slung both weapons over her shoulder with a nod.

Bishop afforded himself one last glance at the thrashing woman on the floor as she frantically attempted to slide the two parts of her face back together. The bloodied flaps slid around her skull as she writhed in pain. Bishop knew he should feel pity for the wretched creature, but as he glanced the flailing body, he felt nothing. He hoped it was professional detachment, but it was more likely satisfaction that justice had been served.

Astrid turned away from the barbarous and callous butcher, her face as cold as the centre of a glacier. "What now?"

"Now?" Bishop flicked the Uzi into automatic fire mode. "Now we kill every fucker between us and freedom."

"And I didn't think it was possible to get any wetter."

Bishop jerked his head towards the furthest door. "Come."

"I'm trying not to."

For a moment in time Astrid and Bishop were united in one goal. And they were glorious.

They cut through the violent mass like a scythe. The two danced in unison, one entwined body, perfectly in sync. Like intimate lovers, each anticipated the other's moves and struck when they would have the greatest effect. The art of their brutality was magnificent.

Firing, hacking, gorging, burning and blasting their way through the bedlam of two warring tribes, they out-gangstered every mafia hardman who had the misfortune to stagger into their path. They showed no mercy. Whether it was Salvo's or Pugliese's men, it didn't matter; all met the business end of their guns and the steel of their blades.

After twenty minutes, they emerged at the front gate, bloodied and exhausted but alive. Without the other, neither would have survived.

The two trod away from the compound, dragging their feet, memory of movement the only thing propelling them forward. They tossed their spent weapons; every bullet had found a home.

Bishop found he had to concentrate to even walk. His body ached for rest, but he knew they weren't done. "Head into town or cross country?" His voice was as broken as his body.

Astrid was equally unsteady, her black cocktail dress slick with the blood of her enemies. "Town, but let's take the back streets, you never know who's calling for rein-forcements. We can beg, borrow or steal a phone. Then we become ghosts."

They limped down the moonlit backstreets of the Italian countryside in silence, their tired footfalls and the occasional bleat of a sheep the only sounds.

Bishop was unsure if their silence was due to exhaus-tion or the fact that they were avoiding talk of what came next. For a brief moment they'd been allies, united in one goal: survival. Now it was a different matter. Bishop still needed Astrid, but that would soon change. It was a deli-cate balancing act. He needed to remind himself that Astrid was Astrid. No matter how glorious the warrior woman appeared with her mussed hair, she was still the enemy. Necessity forced him to side with her, but it was inevitable that the dynamic would change, and soon. Astrid would resort to her usual ways and Bishop would try to bring her to justice. They both knew it was coming.

Under the full moon, Bishop kept Astrid one step ahead of him, a tactically advantageous position. Or at least, that's what he tried to tell himself. It also gave him ample opportunity to bask in her beauty. Underneath the grime, she was still exquisite. With a straight back, she strode forward, the slit down the side of her cocktail dress showing the gloriousness of her slender leg. Her face was smeared with grime and blood, yet her brilliance shone through. Even with the coating of death, she was still stunning.

Bishop's tired mind reeled. *How could someone so wrong cause such conflicting emotions? How could I be so attracted to someone who has wrought so much pain?*

Any second, Bishop expected Astrid to turn on him. For a moment they'd been united by a common foe, but now they were separated, their goals diverged. As if reading his mind, Astrid glanced back and gave him an impish grin. "We should stay together as a team."

Bishop shook his head. "Are you talking now, or forever more?"

"We have a better chance together, you know that. Once we're sure we're free, we can keep up with this extended foreplay you insist on."

Bishop harrumphed. "You started it."

"I most certainly did not."

Placing his fists on his hips, Bishop asked, "Remember the cargo ship? Oslo?"

Astrid blew him a raspberry. "It's always facts with you. Do we have an accord?"

Bishop nodded. He really didn't have much choice. The two strode on in silence. For a while.

"Talking of forever more, my offer still stands." Astrid half turned, but didn't meet his eyes. "We can still run away together. Tell the world to go to hell. All of them. We find an island somewhere, open a bar, raise hell or raise a family. Probably both. We can disappear, Bishop, you and me. We both know how to go off grid. I have enough money for us to become shadows—we can shed who we've been. I guarantee I'd make you happy. We can do it."

Her gaze was focused forward; she didn't glance back. Perhaps she didn't want to see his reaction. Perhaps she didn't want to let him see how much she believed her own words. She strode on.

He wanted to say out loud that she was certifiable. It was a thought he'd had many times, but he no longer felt the conviction he once had. And still, he knew he had to fight taking her proposal seriously.

Bishop attempted to sound impassive. "We'd never work out, Astrid."

She pivoted, glaring. "Where have you been the last few days? We've finally bonded, we've connected, like I always knew we would." She poked him in the chest; he hardly felt it. "Did you not see what we just did, *together*? We were death made manifest. Both of us. We should have been dead, so many times over. There was no way anyone should have survived that, but we did. We." Her finger flicked between the two of them to emphasise the point. "It meant something." Pointing to distant lights, she went on. "It's probably half an hour to walk to the town. Do me the courtesy of at least thinking about it, would you, please?"

In the moonlight, Bishop thought he detected tears welling in her eyes. She turned and marched forward, leaving him in her wake. Despite himself, Bishop did exactly what she asked.

The restaurant owner looked on with a mixture of annoyance and fear. He was just locking his front door when Bishop and Astrid sidled up, pleading to use his phone. Initially disinclined to reopen his establishment, when they stepped into the light and he noticed their bloodied forms, he reluctantly yielded.

Bishop held the phone to his ear as he dialled. The owner seemed mildly alarmed at the sheer number of digits, but said nothing. It was a number Bishop knew by heart. He had to. He waited for five extremely long rings before someone answered.

"Geraldine's Floristry, Franz speaking."

The tiniest of smirks crossed Bishop's lips. "A little late for a florist to be answering the phone, wouldn't you think, Franz?"

"Bloody hell, it's you."

"It is indeed, as you say, me."

"I don't know if you're aware of this, but you're meant to be in a lovely little cottage near Selborne." Paul's tone was even, but Bishop still detected undercurrents. One was relief, the other sheer annoyance at what Bishop had put him through.

"Funny story, I was trying to find my way to the bathroom and got terribly lost."

"That so? And where did you accidentally end up?"

"Italy."

There was a loud exhalation at the other end of the phone. "That may be the most exhaustive wrong turn in history."

"You might be right, Paul, but listen, I've got a lot to tell you, but I have two critical things I need to cover off. First, the mission to Istanbul is compromised."

"You're off that case, mate."

"I thought I was too, but forces," Bishop cast a fleeting look at Astrid, who gazed at the roof with great interest, "pulled me back in."

Astrid's eyes snaked southward. "I do so enjoy pulling."

Bishop scowled at her and went on. "There are forces —I won't say who over an unsecure line—who know our people are there; likely more than one, in fact. The team is in danger. I'll explain why later, but you need to relocate them. Now."

"Consider it done. What was the other thing?"

"Can you call me an Uber?"

The rhythmic thrum of car tyres echoing in the cold night didn't lull Bishop into slumber. It was a long way to Rome, the Royal Marine driver had advised them, but Bishop couldn't rest. It seemed like for every kilometre they travelled, the alliance between he and Astrid unravelled, thread by tiny thread. The further they journeyed from their moment of unity against the world, the closer the cold light of reality became.

After Bishop had hung up from Paul, they'd thanked the annoyed restaurateur and lapsed into a morose silence. They both knew that whatever came next would shatter their partnership and force them into being adversaries once more. It was inescapable.

Beside him, Astrid held her head against the window, eyes closed. In spite of the grime coating her, she seemed peaceful. For the briefest of instants, Bishop wondered what would happen if he leaned over and kissed her. He instantly buried the idea. Deep. There are certain things you just never do in front of Royal Marines.

As if reading his thoughts, Astrid opened her eyes, undid her seatbelt and glided across the back seat. She slid her arm underneath Bishop's and lay her head against his chest. Closing her eyes once more, she remained mute. What was there to say? They knew where this was headed. And it wasn't Rome.

The car hit a bump and Bishop woke with a start. Had he really been asleep? He shielded his eyes against the bright sunlight of dawn. Outside, the car flitted past dilapidated multi-storey buildings skirted by wide, already busy streets. The outskirts of Rome.

They didn't have long.

Still wrapped around his arm, Astrid looked up. "Morning, sleepyhead."

"How long was I out?"

"Long enough for me to steal your wallet and draw a dick on your forehead."

"That long?"

She grinned wide. It was a pleasant moment of stillness.

"Where are they taking us?" Her happy disposition dissolved.

"Rome station. I'm to be debriefed and shot out of a cannon, or whatever the correct protocol is for evading assigned protection."

"And me?" Her voice sounded small.

He fought the urge to shrug. Bishop knew it would be an insufficient answer. In truth, he didn't know. MI6 could hand Astrid over to the Italian police and wash their hands of her. Alternatively, she could be extradited to the UK to face their own legal system. Then again, she could be whisked off under extraordinary rendition and tortured to reveal every last skerrick about her vast illegal arms network and never seen again. It was highly unlikely she'd be put up in a luxury hotel, given ten thousand euros and a VIP tour of the Colosseum.

"I honestly don't know."

Bishop knew the closer they came to their destination, the harder his occupational armour should become. He'd always prided himself on his professional detachment, but at that moment it failed him. He knew it was illogical. He knew it was insane. But he just couldn't bring himself to relish the moment Astrid would be handed over to her fate. Even though it went against every ounce of training he'd ever received, Bishop failed to remain impartial.

"We're not escaping to a tropical island together, are we?" She didn't look at him, instead watching the passing streets. The morning traffic hadn't hit peak yet and they travelled at a good speed, but it was becoming busier by the minute.

"I don't think in this lifetime, no."

"I guess we're going to have to revert to our previous selves, then?"

Bishop went to stroke her hair and stopped himself. "I'm going to posit another nefarious scenario."

She turned to face him, a smirk creasing the edges of her sad face. "Do tell, you cunning linguist."

"You face what's coming. Cooperate. We can see where we're at once you're done. They may lessen your sentence if you—"

"No."

"No?"

"I'm disappointed you'd even think I could." Astrid pulled herself away, slid across the back seat and folded her arms. "That's not who I am, Bishop. That's not who I'll ever be."

"So you won't even contemplate cooperation?"

A wicked grin stretched across her face. "Where's the fun in that?" She pointed in the direction they were travelling. "Is that where we're headed?"

Bishop didn't turn; he didn't fall for the obvious deception. Instead, he watched as Astrid opened the door and, without even looking, leapt out of the moving car.

The Royal Marine's head snapped around, glaring at the open car door. "Fucken' hell!"

He stamped on the brakes, slamming the two men forward and causing more screeches behind. Thankfully no one crashed into them. Both the Royal Marine and

Bishop tore their doors open and raced to the rear of the vehicle. They were on an overpass, another road beneath the bridge they were on.

Car and lorry drivers poked their heads out of their windows and shouted Italian obscenities at the lunatic driver who'd stopped in the middle of the road. Cars sped past on either side, honking their horns and adding to the chaos.

Bishop looked in all directions. There was no sign of Astrid. Beside him, the Royal Marine had his sidearm out and was scanning the streets. Bishop pushed the gun down and shook his head. *She's gone.* They kept searching, but there was no sign of her.

The Royal Marine went to nod in agreement, then stopped. He squinted in confusion and leaned forward, pointing at Bishop's face. "Uh, sir, there's a… there's a mark on your forehead. It's a… you might want to rub it off."

A parting gift. Taking one last scan of the street, Bishop shook his head with a small chuckle and headed back to the car.

Astrid was gone. Bishop had work to do.

# CHAPTER EIGHT

The shouting lasted from morning tea right up until the end of regular business hours. First the station chief, then Paul over conference link, then even the Chief of the Secret Intelligence Service chipped in over the phone, taking time out of her conference in Switzerland. The topic of the discussion varied; his escape from protective guard, neglecting to notify anyone that he'd left protection of his own volition, his traipsing around Europe, ensnaring a foreign intelligence organisation – namely Oleg and the SVR – engaging a known enemy and, last but not least, murdering a good number of Italian nationals on their home soil. The words varied but the sentiment remained the same: Bishop had fucked up. Very very badly.

It was plain to see his career was over. Not even in the dim dark ages of MI6 before the Cambridge Five could the Service allow such behaviour to stand. Regardless, Bishop cooperated fully, telling each successive interviewer the whole, unabashed truth. They seemed particularly interested in the information he was able to supply about the 'Ndrangheta. The only part he left out were his feelings towards Astrid. That detail was for him alone.

In the face of all the yelling, Bishop was relieved the hear the MI6 team in Istanbul had been relocated. The new lead on the mission, Lanaway, was a twat, but he was an MI6 twat. That afforded him all due professional deference. Bishop threw in the additional sarcastic comments for free.

Being MI6's newest persona non grata, Bishop hadn't been given a full mission update on Istanbul, but he'd gleaned enough to put together a rough picture. In spite of good early intelligence, the team in Turkey had failed to locate Yousef Sharif. There had been several unsubstantiated reports of his whereabouts, but they had been unable to find evidence themselves. Either Astrid's people had him well hidden, or Dario Pugliese's people had made their move already.

Bishop had to assume Astrid had survived her flight from the car in Rome. It was unknown if Giuliana Pugliese had survived the massacre. Who else knew about Sharif? Istanbul had always been a den of spies, going back hundreds of years; little had changed. Who knew what other powers were at play?

Not that any of this made a lick of difference. Bishop's career was over. He probably should have been contemplating what came next. Gardener? Taxidermist? Bovine in-vitro fertilisation technician? Who could say? He assumed whatever his next career was, it would be far from the world of frequent brushes with death and constant danger. For all he knew taxidermy fit that bill. Probably. He'd have to look into it.

Bishop sat alone in the empty conference room, slumped in the leather seat. He was spent. He couldn't remember the last decent sleep he'd had. That, and being yelled at for the better part of a day, tends to take it out of you. At that precise moment he didn't actually care what his fate entailed. All he wanted was a soft bed, a pillow and fourteen days of uninterrupted sleep.

"How red raw are those buttocks, Sunshine?"

Glancing around the room, Bishop confirmed he was alone. Then he looked at the large TV at the head of the conference table. Paul's face dominated the screen. He appeared mildly amused.

"I don't think I'll be able to sit down for a week."

Paul frowned. "You're sitting down now."

Too exhausted to offer a witty retort, Bishop waved his hand vaguely in the hope it would suffice.

"I've been making some calls." Bishop knew Paul well enough not to interrupt. "Given the notorious Astrid Spencer is still at large, your intimate knowledge of the Yousef Sharif case and your recent, shall we generously call it an *investigation* of Pugliese's operation, your stupid name kept appearing at the top of the list of those most qualified to lead the Istanbul operation."

Blinking several times, Bishop had to concentrate to realise he wasn't hallucinating. "I'm... you're not firing me?"

Paul sighed, but Bishop detected a hint of amusement. "As much as some pretend otherwise, this is not the Boy Scouts, Bishop. One does not earn merit badges for good deeds and helping little old ladies cross the street. Espionage is a dirty business. We live in a morally grey time and work in an even greyer profession. The information you supplied on the Calabrian mafia was the best intel we've had in ten years. Don't misinterpret me, you fucked up. You fucked up so royally that your ledger will be permanently smeared with your recent transgressions. You'll likely never be promoted. You will forever have the spectre of these events hovering over you at the Service." He sighed. "But no, you're not fired. But let me be exceptionally clear on this: this mission is your last and only chance to minutely redeem yourself. Screw it up and you will be completely done. Do you understand me?"

Bishop gave a hesitant nod. He was unsure if his unlikely redemption was due to Paul's influence or MI6's desperate need. He realised he didn't care. "When do I fly out?"

"There's a car waiting downstairs."

"Outstanding." Bishop stood, feeling suddenly revived.

"Oh, and Bishop?"

"Hmmm?"

"Have a shower and a shave first. You look like hell."

"Yes boss." Bishop issued a genuine smile. "And Paul? Thank you. I realise you must have gone strongly into bat for me and I will be forever grateful. I'll repay you for this, you have my word."

Paul knew the gravity those words held. Bishop wasn't one to make promises he couldn't keep.

Paul nodded. "Sod that. Bring them down. Bring them all down. You manage that, drinks are on me."

"If I do that, I'll bring you a bottle of Glenfarclas 40-Year-Old my bloody self."

Paul gave a considered nod. "The gloves are off for this one. We can't let any of them win. *Any* of them. You understand what that means?"

Bishop did. No prisoners. No quarter. By implication, or perhaps direct order, Astrid Spencer was not to survive.

The Ciragan Palace Kempinski was once a 19th-century Ottoman palace, now a five-star luxury hotel. The lavish, Moorish-influenced hotel room overlooked the bustling shipping lanes of the Strait of Istanbul, the continental boundary between Europe and Asia. Outside, the blue water sparkled in the bright sunshine. Unfortunately, the mood in the room was in stark contrast to the warm, inviting day outside. In fact, it was positively arctic.

Bishop sat cross-legged on a mat in front of a large tiled coffee table. Opposite sat the leader of the MI6 team, David Lanaway. With his neatly trimmed beard and beady dark eyes behind thick black glasses, Bishop always thought he looked like an unemployed folk singer.

On the other side of the table sat Bishop with the remainder of the team, Bridgeman and Fitzherbert. They were his hand-picked squad. Before being tucked away in protective custody, Bishop had taken time to get to know them, hear their experiences, learn how they ticked. More importantly, he'd cultivated a strong team dynamic and forged a tight-knit group.

Lyle Bridgeman, a tall, former Brixton resident of African-Caribbean descent, had been the first to join Bishop's team and brought weapons and tactical knowledge. He and Bishop had bonded over their mutual hatred of the Chelsea Football Club. Penelope Fitzherbert was the tech expert, and originally hailed from Aberdeen. On their first meeting she had made it clear that they could "Go an' boil your heads, ye bawbags, if ye think I'm joinin' some fucken' boys club." Bishop had liked the short, dark-haired firebrand immediately. In the few short weeks they'd known one another, the three had forged a tight camaraderie.

Lanaway was never part of the dynamic. He sat across from the others with his arms folded, and seethed.

Fitzherbert sipped her coffee and closed her eyes in pleasure. "One thing is for certain, this place asparagus-pisses all over the shithole hotel we were in. Pretty sure the rats had pet rats." She took a handful of cashews and poured them into her mouth. "A lass could get used to this."

Bishop smiled. "I take it you haven't found Yousef Sharif yet?"

"Not as yet. We had strong early leads when we arrived," Bridgeman sighed, "but we were directed to first vet out local operatives and contacts. That took time."

Bishop's mouth dropped open. "But the whole point of this mission was that it operated independently. That it aroused no local suspicion."

"Yes, that was our understanding as well," confirmed Bridgeman, "but we were advised that was not a tactically advantageous course of action. By the time we hit the streets the trail had gone cold."

Aghast, Bishop asked, "What lamebrained idiot ordered that?"

Bridgeman's gaze darted to Lanaway. He gave a small shrug. "Not my place to say, sir."

Across the coffee table, Lanaway narrowed his eyes at Bishop. "The jaded assessment of some members of the team is irrelevant." He waved in Bishop's direction. "We've relocated as ordered. Now, if you would be so kind as to give us whatever information you must so you can totter off and leave us to our assignment, that would be most appreciated."

Bishop could see Lanaway's seething resentment boiling just under the surface, but the man's public-school upbringing prevented him from truly expressing what he felt. It was a shame; Bishop was looking forward to the confrontation.

He took his time to finish the small Turkish coffee in front of him. "That's the thing, you see David, I'm not going anywhere." He placed the cup quietly on the table.

"In light of recent developments, I've been ordered to take command of the mission, effective immediately."

Both Bridgeman and Fitzherbert broke into wide grins. Only Bridgeman tried to hide his.

Fitzherbert placed her fists under her chin and glanced between Bishop and Lanaway. "I wish I'd brought popcorn."

Amused, Bridgeman leaned over and spoke quietly. "Shhh. Not helping."

"I won't do it!" Each successive word from Lanaway seemed to get two octaves higher.

Bishop smiled and raised an eyebrow. "You misunderstand me—it wasn't a request." Sparing the man any further humiliation, Bishop went on. "You are still an essential part of the team, David, it's just Vauxhall Cross thought the mission needed someone who's familiar with the historic aspects of the operation and the new intelligence that's come to light."

Bishop wanted to be out in the streets, working the case. Finding Yousef Sharif. Or Astrid. He knew what his personal priority was. Just as equally, he knew this conversation was essential in order for them all to move forward.

"You wait until Paul Cavendish hears of this!" Lanaway must have known he was shrieking.

Bishop fought the urge to smirk. "He's the one who gave the order."

Across the table, Lanaway's mouth flopped open and shut silently. Bishop left him to it and turned to the others.

"I'll need you to present all leads and intel you have by," he glanced at his watch, "fifteen hundred. I want tactical analysis, weapons inventory, capability assessments and local network appraisals at sixteen hundred. Be ready to roll out at eighteen hundred, full kit, surveillance active. The game changes as of now. From here on, we do it my way."

Lanaway snorted. "So we're going to sleep with everyone and let someone else mop up the mess?"

Bishop grinned. "Something like that, yes."

Fitzherbert slapped her hands together. "Sounds good to me." She smiled and turned to Bishop. "What's the priority, sir?"

"We find this son of a bitch to prevent a global economic meltdown."

"And then?"

"Cornettos for everyone."

Fitzherbert grinned. "I fucken love Cornettos."

The team went to work.

It only took a few minutes on the streets of Istanbul for Bishop to know something wasn't right. It wasn't any one thing in particular, more of a thin film coating the entire city. Istanbul was on edge. It was in the eyes of the locals, the way they nervously glanced around the street as if expecting something bad to be waiting around the corner. For all Bishop knew, something was.

"This wasn't in your briefing, Bridgeman." Bishop spoke into the mic on the lapel of his sports coat.

"What's that, boss?"

Bishop smiled at how soon he'd reverted to being the leader of his team. Well, the majority of his team. "Has something spooked the locals? Is there some protest or crackdown going on?"

"Negative, sir. Well, none that's on state-run outlets or social media. As far as we can tell, everything is peachy."

But everything wasn't peachy. Bishop could read it in the faces of the locals: something was up. This was why he always preferred to have assets on the ground instead of an overreliance on technology. It was something the penny-pinching politicians never understood; removing operatives from the field weakened MI6's capabilities. No algorithm could replicate human assessment of a situation. You sensed things in the field, you could read the mood of a place. And right now, he sensed a city on edge, like something was about to explode. Bishop forged onward, attempting to suppress the feeling of unease, but it remained nonetheless.

The last known sighting of Yousef Sharif had been at the Grand Bazaar, but there was no use trying to find him there. Even if he'd never left the Bazaar it would be next to impossible to locate the prince. Five thousand shops, labyrinthine passageways, thousands of tourists, shopkeepers and locals crawling over one another. It would be a monumental task that would send even a team of Where's Wally experts to their knees in despair.

Bishop didn't need a team of Where's Wally experts. He only needed one man: Demir Tekin. Entering the southern entrance of the Grand Bazaar, the MI6 agent made his way through its tangled walkways. The sweet stench of spices, the shouting vendors, the colourful trinkets; the chaotic nature of the place could be discombobulating to the uninitiated.

Zeroing in on Demir's location, Bishop became increasingly pissed at Lanaway. Not only had he blown the secrecy of the operation by broadcasting to any intelligence organisation he could find, he had completely neglected to exploit their single most valuable asset. Whether that was because Demir was not strictly from the intelligence community or because he had been personally cultivated by Bishop was unknown. Either way, it was another manifestation of Lanaway's incompetence.

Entering the perfume store, Bishop was overcome by a cacophony of scents. Tiny unlabelled bottles lined the walls. Demir was seated behind the counter quietly fanning himself as he read the newspaper. Middle-aged and balding, he'd managed to stay relatively thin, but Bishop detected a few extra pounds since their last meeting. On seeing Bishop, Demir leapt from his wicker throne and threw his arms open wide.

"Dost!" Grin as wide as his arms, he embraced Bishop so hard he knocked the wind out of him. "Bishop, my friend! This is an unexpected surprise for such a humble merchant."

Bishop did his best not to laugh out loud. Demir Tekin was many things, but two things he certainly wasn't were humble and merely a merchant.

Motioning for his guest to take a seat, Demir's smile remained firmly in place. "Tea?"

Bishop smiled and nodded. This was Demir's way. Tea first, business second. Even if he ran into Demir's store under a hail of bullets, he suspected he'd have to wait until after the first glass of tea before Demir would offer shelter.

"Thank you, Demir."

Extracting two gold-gilded glasses, the host poured tea. The pot was already boiled, as if he'd expecting Bishop. He most likely had. They sipped the heady brew for a while.

"How are your daughters?"

Demir sighed theatrically. He always made a song and dance about his offspring. It was plain he loved them dearly, but they were a reliable source of animated conversation.

He threw his hands in the air. "They will be the death of me! What did I do for God to bestow four such creatures on a frail man such as myself? All of them marrying age, all trying to kill me in different ways. Sometimes I think it would be easier, Bishop, if I died and did not have to worry about what homeless bum will break their hearts after stealing my dowry."

Bishop nodded, there was nothing to be said. He shrugged and sipped his tea. Then there was a shift in Demir's disposition; his shoulders drew back and his face grew stern. The small talk seemed to be over.

Bishop took his cue. "My friend, I apologise if I'm rushing you, but I'm here on important business. I'm here to find—"

"I do not know where he is."

Bishop smiled. "No, I didn't suppose it would be that easy. But perhaps you could assist us in getting back on track?"

"I would have thought I'd done that already?" Demir took a sip of tea and cocked an eyebrow. "But it was so long ago, it is very hard to recall." His words dripped with derision.

Bishop had to concede he had a point. After all, it was Demir who had supplied MI6, Bishop in particular, with the picture of Yousef Sharif walking the streets of the Grand Bazar.

"My apologies. The photograph your man took was extremely helpful, and we acted as fast as MI6 could in such circumstances, but there were... complications. Especially for me. I apologise we did not arrive sooner."

Demir leaned in and examined Bishop's face. "Woman troubles, my friend?"

"No." Bishop sighed. "Well, yes, but not what you're thinking."

"You are truly an amazing man to know my thoughts at all times, I think?"

That earned him a smile. "Fair call. I'm sorry I was slow to act."

His host shrugged. "Maybe next time I go to another foreign power, hmmm? The Israelis pay ridiculous sums for this type of information, do they not?" He slapped Bishop on the shoulder. "I am joking, of course". His tone was convivial, but there was an undercurrent. *We are fine, but don't fuck me around again.* Bishop had no intention of doing so. Thankfully, Demir's demeanour brightened and he was soon back to his jovial self. "What is it I can do for you?"

"First, a question if I may."

"Anything for you."

"What's going on in the city? Everyone seems tense. There's something going on, the place is a powder keg."

Demir gave him a slow wizened nod. "You have seen, hmmm?" He rubbed his stubbled chin. "I suppose a spy would notice these things. The popular local governor had been forcibly replaced. The national government had banned protests, which was ironic, as it made many people protest. Everyone is on edge. Something is, as your Sherlock Holmes would say, afoot. But no one is quite sure what that it is. There are many rumours, however."

"There always are."

Demir gave a nod. "But nothing of substance, I am afraid. Or at least not as far as I have been able to ascertain."

More to himself than Demir, Bishop nodded. That just added further complications to an already chaotic situation.

Finishing his tea, Demir placed the glass carefully on his ornate table. "I return to my previous question. What can I do for you, my friend?"

Bishop laid out what he needed from his old friend and, more importunately, where it would end. Or at least, where he wanted it to end. There were so many moving parts to his plan, it was likely one would fly off and destabilise the whole thing. It was a gamble, a calculated one, playing on how well Bishop read people, anticipated their moves given the right motivation. If he were honest, a lot hinged on whether he knew Astrid better than she knew herself. Bishop kept that part to himself.

For the first time he glimpsed a crack in his host's bearing. Demir blinked several times and assessed the man across the table with concern in his eyes. "I mean this with the utmost respect…" He leaned over and placed his hand over Bishop's. "You are completely unhinged?"

Giving his host a cheeky grin, Bishop nodded and placed his own glass on the table. "Yes, my friend. I am."

"I've always stated you were quite mad." Demir gave an amused shake of his head. "I never truly believed it until now."

"No one is going to argue the point."

Demir shrugged. "Where do we begin?"

A sneer crossed Bishop's lips. "Let the bastards know where they can come and kill me."

## CHAPTER NINE

Knowing exactly which bastard Bishop was referring to was the problem. Astrid Spencer could still have Sharif, but Dario Pugliese could just as likely have taken him by now. Equally, Giuliana Pugliese's people might be in possession of the Saudi prince. Or he may have been spirited away to a far-off land. Or dead. He could be wearing a tutu and learning the tuba in Azerbaijan for all Bishop knew.

Without having been asked, the waiter slapped another coffee on the table in front of Bishop, interrupting his thoughts. The black liquid slopped onto the white tablecloth and the cup threatened to tip over, but remained upright. The swarthy waiter didn't apologise or offer to clean up. The hoity man had a long, predatory nose and fingers that were too long, giving the impression of a spider. He went about his serving duties with the same grim face Bishop wore, seemingly oblivious to the half empty coffee he'd served. Bishop shrugged. People took coffee too seriously. He could never be with someone who obsessed over coffee.

Sipping his half empty, lukewarm beverage, Bishop

took in the sightseers and families sauntering around Sultanahmet Square. It was a wide square with a smattering of trees, the odd stolen Egyptian obelisk and several souvenir stalls. The bright midday sun illuminated a picturesque scene. Bishop's outside seat at the café afforded him views of the remnants of the old hippodrome and the historic and striking Blue Mosque, as well as the massive Hagia Sophia, a triumph of Byzantine architecture. It was a beautiful setting for the ugliest of endeavours.

Bishop's immediate plan was to have Demir tell the local underworld where they could find Bishop on a Tuesday afternoon. The 'humble merchant' certainly had the connections. The mafia had their fingerprints on organised crime in every major city in the world, and Istanbul was no exception. Having Demir broadcast the information wouldn't be difficult. Keeping Bishop alive once he did so certainly would.

And broadcast, Demir certainly did. Demir told each and every one of his criminal contacts 'confidentially' who Bishop was and where he could be found. They may as well have gone to the paint store and emblazoned a giant target on his back. There was a fear that advertising Bishop's presence may have attracted more than just Astrid and the various Pugliese factions. That was a risk they'd have to take.

Bishop's plan was to get the mafia to create a racket. Astrid and her goons should follow—if they were in the city, that was. Exactly which part of the mafia was another unknown. Giuliana Pugliese had been taken down, but she hadn't been eliminated. She could still be alive, or even be in Istanbul, though it was doubtful. It would be difficult to travel after your face had been sliced in two. Her brother was in Istanbul, and may have secured Sharif already; that was yet another unknown component of an already unsteady engine.

Astrid's plan was to manipulate Sharif into influencing the rest of the OPEC board to change the price of oil to one that would benefit Astrid. She'd know the outcome, which would ensure she could make the right investments at the most opportune time. Who knew what Dario's plan was? More of the same, or his own spin on it? Bishop couldn't fathom. The head of the Calabrian mafia could have perpetuated Astrid's scheme for his own purposes or rigged the game to do just the opposite. Either way, it couldn't succeed. The world was unstable enough already, it didn't need individuals blackmailing the head of OPEC and plunging the world into financial chaos.

If Astrid and her minions still had Yousef Sharif, Bishop had no way of contacting her. This was the next best thing. Causing a stir within the underworld would certainly garner her attention. He was counting on Astrid being Astrid. Her natural state was to act, sometimes impulsively, especially where Bishop was concerned. He was gambling that he knew her better than she knew herself. The danger was, the reverse could equally be true.

As was Bishop's way, he would act and make the rest up as he went along. Although this time he did so more cautiously. He had a team to look after; his recklessness could have consequences. It was a balancing act. On a highwire. Over a pit of crocodiles. And the rope was on fire. As Bishop finished the blandest tourist coffee twenty lira could buy, he concluded he hadn't brought enough underwear for this mission.

Around Sultanahmet Square, members of his team were placed at strategic intervals, affording them vantagepoints on all approaches. The plan would work if their rivals wanted to take care of Bishop up close and personal. If they decided to take him out with a sniper's bullet, however, it didn't matter how well-positioned Bishop's people were, he was a dead man.

Bishop wasn't one for waiting, yet that was exactly what he'd been doing for the last hour and a half. Being bait wasn't the most exciting of undertakings. He could only sit on a coffee for so long before the disinterested waiter would ask him to move along. Just as he was considering whether he should order a side of fries, a voice spoke into his ear.

"Heads up," Fitzherbert said cheerfully from her position at a park bench a hundred metres away, in the corner of the square. "There's a suspicious looking character approaching from the south. He's definitely up to something, waddling in a most shady manner."

Grinning, Bishop whispered into his lapel mic. "Waddling?"

Bishop could almost hear the grin over the comms. "Fine, it's a duck. There's a suspicious looking duck approaching. Be on your guard."

His team were just as bored as he was. Well, most of them.

"Fitzherbert, stow the useless chatter."

If he wasn't so concerned about drawing attention to himself, Bishop would have chastised Lanaway for using real names over comms. He seemed determined to make up for his newfound lack of authority with over-officiousness and unhindered contempt. Bishop half expected Fitzherbert and Bridgeman to either ignore him, punch the guy, or launch a violent mutiny.

"It's not useless." Fitzherbert's voice went up two octaves. "Have a look at him. The dude's definitely up to something, I'd put money on it. He's shifty as fuck."

"Fitzherbert!" Lanaway's voice joined his former

subordinate in the upper octave range. "I will put you on report if you don't mind the language."

There was a pause, followed by a deep sigh. "Yes, *David.*"

Somehow Fitzherbert made 'David' rhyme with 'twat'.

*This is going well,* Bishop thought to himself. Lanaway sat in a car at the edge of the park, ready if they required a quick getaway. Fitzherbert was located at the opposite end of the square to Lanaway, sitting in a restaurant over-looking the plaza, as well as the adjacent main road. Bridgeman was between them, wandering between points of interest. Bishop had overheard him twice having to fend off requests by the locals to sit or let them buy him a drink.

If he were completely honest, Bishop didn't want Lanaway anywhere near the actual operation in case he interfered. No doubt the rest of the team was behind him on that. Bishop sensed it was a sentiment Lanaway was fully aware of.

"Uh, guys, heads up."

Bishop sighed. As quietly as he could, he said, "If this is another duck…"

"Ducks don't have legs like this. Or blonde hair. Or… you never said she had such a sweet arse, Bishop."

"Fitzherbert!" Lanaway sounded like he was about to storm out of the car.

"I have visual." Bishop most certainly did.

It wasn't hard to find the target Fitzherbert had identi-fied. Strolling confidently across the pale concrete flag-stones on the other side of the square, the woman cut a striking figure. In a short floral dress, knee-high leather boots and a wide-brimmed sun hat, she sashayed across the square as if it were a fashion runway. Passers-by stared with jealousy or admiration. Some just outright ogled. Astrid seemed oblivious to the attention and made a beeline for her destination. Bishop.

As he watched Astrid from a distance, the shadow of someone much closer lurched over him. Initially Bishop leaned forward to avoid the figure beside him. That was, until the person spoke.

"A good spy hides in the shadows and does not, I am told, shout his presence like an idiot, Englishman."

Looking up, Bishop's mouth dropped open in genuine shock.

"Bloody hell, where did that dude come from?" Fitzherbert's voice was caked in surprise.

Bishop didn't reply, although he knew the answer. The new arrival was adept at sneaking up on people. Spies tend to be.

Recovering quickly, Bishop scowled. "You can't be here, Oleg."

The big man sat with a thud and harrumphed. "Oh, I am so glad to see you, Oleg. How have you been, Oleg? I am so sorry I left you on that shitty boat on the Venetian harbour, especially when you had broken ribs, Oleg."

"Oh, that guy." Fitzherbert blew out air. "Sorry he got through, boss. Wonder who else is going to crash this party?"

"I am not glad to see you, Englishman."

"Yes, yes, fine." Bishop spied Astrid far in the distance, drawing closer by the second. Had Oleg seen her? "If you're done, I suggest you get out of here."

The Russian shrugged. "Oh, I am sorry, do you have exclusivity over Istanbul? I was not aware, my apologies."

"This guy's complicating things." Fitzherbert sounded like she was changing position. "Do you need assistance?"

"Stand down. Oleg's an old…"

The SVR agent smirked. "Friend would be lie, would it not, Englishman?"

Not wanting to concede the point, Bishop changed the subject. "Look, I don't know how you found me, but there's far more at play than you know."

Oleg nodded and motioned to the waiter, indicating that he wanted the same coffee as Bishop. The Russian appeared unperturbed that Bishop was speaking to his team remotely. For all Bishop knew, Oleg could be doing the same.

"I was already in the city on the trail of our mutual friend when Russian intelligence…" Oleg paused. "Best in the world", they both chimed together.

Over comms, Fitzherbert said, "Hey!"

The two spies shared the briefest of smiles before Oleg went on. "They picked up chatter about some fool telling the criminal underworld he was an MI6 spy looking for a wayward Saudi prince. I thought, there's only one idiot in the world who could be that stupid." He spread his arms wide. "And here we are, idiot."

Bishop sighed. "Funny."

Oleg's face hardened as he leaned forward. "You know what else is funny, Englishman?" He tilted his head. "You were my friend when you needed SVR assistance to track the head of Kali, but as soon as I was no longer useful, you—literally—abandoned me." He raised an eyebrow, challenging Bishop to say otherwise. "You did not even contact me to tell me you were not dead. You just disappeared. No, I think you are right, we are not friends, are we Bishop?"

The man had a point.

Bishop watched Astrid get closer. "You don't know what you're involving yourself in, Oleg."

"I know exactly why I am here." Opening his jacket, he showed Bishop his shoulder holster and the MP-443

Grach within. He turned and was unsurprised to see Astrid twenty metres away. He turned back. "And she will pay for what she has done." His hand rested on his pistol.

There was no avoiding the inevitable. Bishop had run out of time. Astrid strolled up to the café and, without asking, sat down at the table.

She turned to Bishop and grinned sweetly. "You brought friends. How sweet." Astrid's radiant smile illuminated the already bright day. "Oleg, always a pleasure."

Bishop turned to the Russian and pushed his hand away from the gun. "You need to go, Oleg."

Oleg's steely eyes bore into Astrid. "I will not leave until I have what I came for."

Astrid let out a sultry chuckle. "Oh boys, no need to fight, there's plenty of me to go round."

Oleg growled. "I should do you here in front of everyone."

On the comms, Fitzherbert choked.

Amused dimples creasing her cheeks, Astrid turned to Bishop. "He still has that inuendo thing happening?"

Bishop shrugged. "He's like a big perplexed inappropriate machine."

If Bishop was hoping humour would crack Oleg's angry façade, he was sorely mistaken. If anything, he grew even more livid.

The big Russian growled, "I should kill you right now in broad daylight."

"Come now, the night we spent together wasn't that bad, was it?" A wicked grin creased Astrid's red lips. "In fact, I distinctly remember the three of us had the most pleasant of times."

"Hang on, *the three of us*?" There was confusion in Bridgeman's voice. "What sort of clip joint is this?"

Bishop ignored the chatter.

Oleg forged on. "You sold weapons to the enemy in Crimea. Many of my brothers in the 31st Guards Air Assault Brigade were killed in their beds because of your greed." His anger bubbled to the surface; he clenched his fists. "I am here to avenge my countrymen."

Bishop knew there was more to it. Oleg had hinted that SVR had ordered Astrid dead. He was here to assassinate her. The situation was becoming more unstable by the second.

"Am I interrupting?"

All three heads turned. Both Astrid and Bishop gasped, while Oleg remained as mute as a statue of Lenin.

Before them stood an unsteady woman. Held up by a cane, she looked damaged and frail, almost. Her expression was anything but weak. It was full of fire and rage.

Oleg's head turned from the disfigured newcomer to Bishop and then to Astrid, his expression moving from confusion to disgust and then anger, in that order.

Giuliana Pugliese sat down at the end of the table opposite Bishop and scowled. No longer possessing the elegant poise she'd once had, she was hunched and mutilated. Her face was a mess of bandages, blackened stitches and red raw skin, not entirely in the place it once was. The raw diagonal scar across her face was a permanent reminder of where Bishop had hacked away the last vestiges of her beauty. Only one eye appeared to be working, the other sat drooping and lifeless. It was like a scene from a horror movie, and Pugliese was the insane slasher.

"You will die today, Bishop of MI6." Her spittle-laden words were coated in venom.

So she finally knew who he was. It seemed Bishop's plan had worked. Glancing around the table at his companions—an angelically calm Astrid, an enraged Pugliese and a fiery but slightly confused Oleg—Bishop thought perhaps his plan had worked a little too well. There were too many players on the field, too many variables, and he had no idea who had the ball.

"Uh, Bishop... what's going on?" Fitzherbert's voice was full of confusion. Little wonder. Bishop was having trouble keeping up himself, and he knew all the competitors. "It's seeming like the Legion of Doom over there. When does Lex Luthor turn up?"

Bishop ignored his colleague. "Isn't this fun?" He clapped his hands together. "Should I order a trio of dips? Who's hungry?"

From the corner of his eye Bishop noticed the waiter approach. It was as if he'd heard what Bishop had said. Perhaps he wasn't as inept as he seemed.

Eyes ablaze, Pugliese reached into her purse and extracted a pistol. With the speed of a whip, she drew and aimed. But she didn't aim at Bishop. Nor was her weapon pointed at Astrid or Oleg. She aimed the pistol in the face of the waiter.

The corners of Pugliese's mouth hardened. "It's been a while... brother."

All heads turned to the previously unremarkable waiter. Standing between Bishop and Astrid, the waiter pulled his own gun and aimed it at his sister across the table. In retrospect, he did possess a somewhat Italian complexion, and bore more than a passing resemblance to Bishop's former captor. The MI6 agent could have kicked himself for not suspecting him earlier.

"Beloved sister. You've never looked more beautiful." His words were hard as granite.

Pugliese's one good eye narrowed. "I'm here for what is rightfully mine."

"And I am here to give it to you." Her brother

nodded. "It is right here in the barrel of this gun. Would you like to see it?"

Impossibly, the situation had become exponentially worse, and Bishop was no closer to the truth. If this descended into a shooting match, Yousef Sharif was as good as dead and the world would tumble into financial chaos. Bishop had seconds to prevent a global meltdown. He had to handle the situation with delicacy, diplomacy and tact.

"Put the guns down you Italian wankers."

All eyes turned to Bishop. No guns were lowered. He sighed.

"I just have one question. Who has Sharif?"

Assessing every face, the two closest to him gave away the answer. The tiniest smirk crossed Dario's lips. Equally, the thinnest sliver of annoyance creased the flawless features on Astrid's face.

"You killed a lot of my people last night," Astrid snarled at Dario, lips pursed. "You'll pay for that."

The Italian shrugged. "I normally abhor killing women, but I will make two exceptions today."

Bishop held up conciliatory palms. "Nobody needs to be shot today."

"I do not agree, Englishman." Oleg's hand delved into his jacket as he snarled at Astrid. "Someone needs to get it today."

"Oh, Oleg," Astrid smiled coyly, "you remember how I love it. That's sweet."

Enraged, Oleg whisked out a pistol at the exact instant Astrid did. She matched his move perfectly and the two sat on either side of the table with guns drawn on one another, just as the two Puglieses were. Everyone at the table radiated homicide. The air stank of death.

Bishop rose to his feet. "Everybody just calm the fuck down!"

But everyone did not calm the fuck down.

In fact, everyone aggravated the fuck up.

Dario's gun was aimed at his sister, but he kept his gaze on Astrid, who sat to his right. Oleg's gun was aimed across the table, directly at Astrid's head. Her gun, in response, was trained on Oleg's chest. Pugliese's pistol in her shaky hand remained trained on her brother.

Oleg was to Bishop's left, Dario to his right. To *his* right, Astrid sat rigidly upright. Pugliese was seated opposite Bishop, but her hand was starting to droop, as if the gun was too heavy for her to keep aloft. Each and every one of them had murder in their eyes. Each looked ready to fire. They were a fraction of a second away from a bloodbath.

"Bishop." Fitzherbert's voice was highly concerned. "You need to get out of there."

It was too late. Everyone knew it. There was only one way it would end.

The bullets flew.

# CHAPTER TEN

Bishop spotted the twitch of Dario's spider finger first. The minutest of gestures translated to the most brutal of outcomes. The Italian fired.

His sister was hit and reeled backwards, firing harmlessly into the air as she did. She screamed, and her gun flew into the far behind her. Pugliese landed hard, out of Bishop's line of sight on the other side of the table.

Bishop didn't hesitate. He acted as brutally as he knew how. Everything happened at once.

His right hand darted out and grasped Dario's wrist, smashing it into the table. Dario fired, and the bullet took a chunk out of a nearby chair. At the same instant, Bishop's left foot shot out, kicking Oleg in his broken ribs. The big Russian screamed in pain and crumpled to the ground. As Bishop continually beat Dario's hand hard against the table to dislodge the weapon, he turned to Astrid and yelled, "Run!"

Astrid didn't need to be told twice. She pivoted and sprinted into the open space of Sultanahmet Square, running for her life, just as Bishop had suggested. Smart girl.

Bishop kept smashing Dario's firing hand on the table to free the pistol. The Italian finally let out a pained cry as the weapon clattered across the table and onto the ground. Laying in kidney punches, Bishop did his best to subdue Dario. But that wasn't his main concern.

With an enraged howl, Oleg hoisted his damaged body upright and aimed his pistol at the fleeing Astrid. She was weaving between scattering tourists, who were fleeing the gun battle themselves. Oleg fired. It was an unfocused shot, high and wide. He wiped a tear from his eye and retargeted.

"Civilians!" Bishop shout was as loud as the shots themselves.

With a scathing expression, Oleg turned to Bishop, then towards the panicked crowd. Astrid didn't miss a stride, and kept racing towards an exit on the far side of the square. Oleg looked at the terrified crowd and lowered his weapon.

Turning, Bishop saw Dario scramble away, but he wasn't in a position to chase him. A big-armed Russian monopolised his attention.

With steam emanating from his ears, Oleg stabbed a finger at Bishop. "You and I will have a reckoning, Englishman. We are not done, do you understand? This is not over."

Without waiting for a response, he stumbled after Astrid, holding his ribs as he went. Bishop had to let him go. He'd already risked so much protecting Astrid, yet again. Bishop could justify his actions all he wanted, claiming he'd saved her so she could be brought in and interrogated on MI6's terms, but he knew there was far more to it. It was a truth he wasn't ready to face.

Shaking loose thoughts he didn't need just then, Bishop rounded the table before Dario had a chance to recover. He knew the mobster's discarded gun was on the other side of the table, along with the body of his sister. When Bishop reached the other side, he found both the gun and Pugliese. Unfortunately, one was in the hand of the other.

Her shoulder was a mass of red; her brother's bullet must have passed through the brachial plexus. Unlike in the movies, it wasn't an injury you shook off and pushed through. She had most likely lost arm function, but wouldn't bleed to death if the bullet hadn't struck the brachial artery. Given the painkillers she was probably on, Pugliese may have been in a better position to deal with it than most. Not that it helped Bishop any.

Taking aim at Bishop with a shaky hand and a cloudy eye, Pugliese looked close to passing out. It seemed her hatred was the only thing keeping her conscious.

Moving as fast as he could, Bishop ducked under Pugliese's aim and hoisted her firing arm skyward. She moved far slower than she would have a few weeks ago. Pugliese fired every bullet she had into the air while screaming like a banshee. Bishop punched her bloodied shoulder. She screamed in pain and collapsed, her last remnants of energy spent on a fruitless attempt at revenge.

In a frail voice, the would-be global criminal master-mind's words were strained. "What did I do to deserve you?"

Bishop stared at her in astonishment for a moment. "Let's start with putting heads on spikes and go from there, shall we?"

Not waiting for her response, Bishop scuttled behind Pugliese to pick up the gun she'd dropped behind her when her brother took his shot. Grabbing the Browning, Bishop's thoughts turned to the head of the 'Ndrangheta. Having recovered from Bishop's savage blows, Dario limped towards what he thought was the safety of

Sultanahmet Square. Hobbling, he attempted to merge himself with the thinning crowd.

Bishop grinned. "Oh, I think not."

"Oi, ya big roaster!" Bishop turned to see Fitzherbert running towards him. Nearing his position, the young Scot was flushed. "What the hell is going on?"

Instinctively, Bishop reached for his earpiece. It was hanging loose on his shoulder; it must have become dislodged during the first struggle. His team had probably been screaming bloody murder and he hadn't heard a word of it. Bishop slotted it in his ear and nodded his thanks.

He pointed to the prone Pugliese. "Patch her up then detain her."

Fitzherbert shook her head in confusion. "Detain her for what?"

Bishop glanced at the whimpering woman. "Everything."

Frowning in acquiescence, Fitzherbert asked, "Where are you going?"

Bishop broke into a run and spoke into his lapel mic. "I'm going after the only man who knows where Sharif is. If we lose him, all this has been for nothing."

Bridgeman's voice came on the line. "Moving to your position, boss." He panted, indicating he was running. "Give me a description of the target."

"He's Italian and dressed as a waiter."

"This thing is making less sense by the minute," Bridgeman panted. "I have visual on him. On it. I see you too. Let's get the fucker."

Bishop caught sight of Bridgeman as he ran into his peripheral view. The two ran after their prey.

"Oh, Bishop?"

It was Lanaway's voice. Bishop had forgotten he was even part of the team.

"I'm a bit busy right now."

"Oh, fine, fine, you keep doing whatever you're doing." There was a distinct smugness to his tone. "You can thank me later."

"Thank you?" Bishop experienced a sudden sense of dread. "For what?"

"I have Astrid Spencer under arrest." He virtually squeed. "She's standing right in front of me."

Bishop stopped running. "You don't know what you're doing, David. She's a most dangerous individual. You have no idea what she's capable of. You really don't."

"Not so inept am I now, hey Bishop? While you were busy having threesomes the rest of us actually attended spy school."

"Lanaway, she's far more dangerous than you realise. You need to—"

"Oh, please!" There was anger now. "I have a gun on her. I'm not a fool."

"David, she's armed. Did you disarm her?"

By way of response, a single gunshot rang out. Nobody in Bishop's team spoke. There was a deafening silence. Finally, a scuffling could be heard, like fabric rubbing against a mic.

Then a voice came on the channel. It was soft and sultry.

"Sorry, lover, have to dash. See you on that island in another life, yeah?"

Bishop heard the faint footfalls of Astrid running away. Unable to take the time to process what had just occurred, Bishop broke into a run. He had someone to catch.

∼

Legs like pistons, Bishop ran as fast as his body could carry him. He hadn't been on the running track for weeks, but his years of training weren't wasted. He wove through the crowd at speed, never slowing, never tiring. He had the target in sight.

"Man… you… gotta… slow… down…" Bridgeman was a well-built man. The strain of his t-shirts indicated substantial hours put in at the gym. But he struggled to keep Bishop's pace. He probably missed leg day.

"I have visual on the target. I'm not slowing, for anyone." Bishop sprinted past a group of police arriving too late, heading the wrong way and ill-prepared for what awaited them. Bishop kept speaking into his comms mic. "You keep up. Don't tell me you never hit the treadmill at the MI6 gym?"

"Screw… you."

Bishop's goading worked; Bridgeman picked up his pace. They narrowed the gap on their prey. If he were honest, Bishop had contemplated pursuing Astrid. Oleg was a damn fine spy and his vendetta against her was personal. He would pursue her relentlessly. But Bishop couldn't save her, not this time.

"Guys." It was Fitzherbert, her voice grave. "I'm… I'm back at the car with Pugliese."

Bishop didn't want to hear the answer, but knew he had to ask the question. "And?"

"Lanaway's dead." She gulped. "Shot through the heart. A clean kill."

At least Astrid had been merciful in her execution. Lanaway was a twat, but he didn't deserve to die like that. It was something Bishop would have to grapple with later.

"Get out of here. You need to leave David's body. The police will be there in seconds. You can't handle Pugliese and get him into the car in time. Take her to the safe house, patch her up as best you can and then wait for us."

"How will you two get there?"

Bishop ran on. "We'll find our own way. Now, go!"

Dario was in sight, running through a park adjacent to the Sea of Marmara. Bishop had to wonder why he hadn't had more men with him at the café. The only conclusion was that Dario's men were already stretched thin protecting Sharif, and he thought he could take Bishop alone. He must have expected Astrid to mount reprisals, so needed to protect his new asset.

Thankfully Dario's crisp white shirt stood out in the fleeing crowd. Bishop hoped the mafia don didn't have a waiting speedboat. Bridgeman struggled to keep up thirty metres behind. Rounding a corner where the expanse of the sea came into view, Dario slowed. The move put Bishop on edge. The bastard was up to something.

Slowing to a walk before completely stopping, Dario turned to his pursuers with a smug leer.

"Heads up, Bridgeman. We're on."

"On?" He panted. "On… what?"

There was no need to say anything because the answer walked out from behind trees on either side of the path. Heavy-set and with noses that had been broken more times than the front row of an inept rugby team, the two mafia henchmen sneered as they raised their revolvers. It seemed Dario wasn't alone after all. The mafia boss was talking, but the wind made it impossible to hear his words. Bishop was unsure if he was issuing orders or addressing his pursuers. Not that it mattered; the results would be the same.

The two henchmen fired. The distance was a challenge, but not impossible for a decent marksman. The target could still be taken down with careful aim and measured breathing. But the two mafia thugs possessed neither of these things. Their footwork was appalling and their shots rushed. The bullets went flying overhead. They may as well have been six-year-olds firing at tin ducks at the fair.

Now it was Bishop's turn.

Leaning into a crouched stance, Bishop extracted his pistol and in a smooth, unhurried motion loosed six shots. Each of the heavies was graced with one head shot and two to the chest, a gift he extended only to the most deserving of recipients. The two men collapsed backwards and thudded lifelessly on the concrete path.

The screaming of the crowd intensified. Thinking they were running from the carnage, they had inadvertently run towards more. They scattered.

Like the big tough mafia hardman he was, Dario Pugliese screamed a high-pitched squeal. He no longer appeared smug. In fact, he looked like a terrified child. He fell to his knees and raised his hands in surrender. With tears streaming down his face, he babbled his capitulation through sobs.

Bridgeman strolled up besides Bishop, winded. "Nice shooting, boss. Now what?"

Grasping Dario by the scruff of the neck, Bishop hoisted him up and pushed the mafia head forward.

He addressed his subordinate. "Search the two bodies for car keys. We'll meet Fitzherbert at the safe house and then…" Bishop smirked.

Bridgeman frowned in confusion. "Then… what?"

"I just love family reunions, don't you?"

The screaming match lasted a good half an hour. It was lucky the basement of the safe house was soundproofed.

Even then, Bishop wasn't sure the walls could contain the ear-piercing shrieks from the Pugliese siblings. As soon as Bridgeman tossed the bound Dario onto the floor, the patched-up Giuliana Pugliese had started shrieking at her brother. In return, Dario spat noxious insults in Italian, English and whatever else was at hand.

The siblings' ear-piercing squabble persisted while both were tied to chairs and positioned at either ends of the basement, and showed no sign of abating. Bishop sighed. He jerked his head towards the stairs and Bridgeman and Fitzherbert followed. They went for tea and biscuits. When they returned, the brother and sister were still at it, but far hoarser than when they'd begun.

"Right, you two!" Bishop managed to drown out the warring siblings for a moment. "Enough of your shenanigans. We're here for answers."

"I'm not telling you anything." Dario spat on the floor. "Incazzarsi, you finocchio testa di cazzo!"

With a slow inhale, Bishop rocked on his heels. "Charming."

Without uttering another word, Bishop strode up to Dario and threw every ounce of his anger into a right hook. It was a good one. The mob boss's seat toppled as he went flying, as did his front tooth. It landed with a clink at his sister's feet. Pugliese looked up from the bloodied incisor and grinned. Dario, on the other hand, looked up at his captor with genuine fear. There was nothing like dislodging dental work to garner one's attention.

"Now." Bishop pushed Dario's chair upright and gave him a pat on the cheek, which made him wince. "We're here for answers. Let's get started, shall we?" His head swivelled between the brother and sister. "You two like to compete, right? Fine, let's play a game, shall we? It's called 'whoever tells Bishop the most gets to live'. The rules are self-explanatory. Who wants to go first?"

The two Puglieses stared at him in abject horror. Bishop casually sat cross-legged between them, gently stroking the Heckler & Koch USP in his hands. He raised an eyebrow in anticipation.

"You are MI6. There are rule you must follow. You will not kill us, British."

Dario spoke without conviction. He didn't believe the words tumbling from his bloodied mouth. He wished he did, but all the fight had been beaten from him.

Sagely, Bishop nodded. "Rules? You're right. There are rules." He paused. "But I'm intrigued. Tell me, oh so clever Dario, what are those rules you seem so familiar with?" Receiving an anxious, blank expression in return, Bishop went on. "To what extent am I allowed to torture, you mean? Can I remove your fingernails with pliers and water torture you until you drown, is that it? Or do you mean am I licenced to kill you in this filthy basement? Do the rules change when a member of our team is murdered in the streets like a dog?"

Bishop's anger grew. He witnessed the two recoil at his ratcheted-up fury. But in this instance, it wasn't directed at them; it was aimed at himself. Lanaway had died due to Bishop's awry mission. Worse, it was Astrid who had pulled the trigger. The woman Bishop had saved on numerous occasions had slain a member of his team. If he hadn't prevented Oleg from taking the shot, Lanaway would still be alive.

He knew he should feel more remorse, but Bishop couldn't summon the requisite emotions. No matter how hard he tried, he couldn't summon the regret he should feel. Perhaps it was the fatigue and adrenaline fighting within his system. But he knew better.

Bishop still didn't know if he would ever be able to

give Paul that bottle of Glenfarclas 40-Year-Old; his promised price for bringing Astrid down. He didn't know if he'd ever walk into Paul's office and place the bottle on his boss's desk. Perhaps one day, but he found it hard to imagine the day he'd take pleasure in Astrid's demise.

Dismissing the wayward thoughts, Bishop forged on with the siblings, who knew nothing of his inner turmoil. "I mean, espionage is illegal under international law, and is punishable by death in Turkey." Neither of those things were true, but Bishop wagered Dario wouldn't know it. He swivelled to face the terrified Italian. "I don't think you need to worry about legalities, my friend." He picked up the automatic pistol and scratched the side of his head. "I think the only thing you need to concern yourself with is what you're going to tell me in the next five minutes, and whether you'll be alive at the end of it."

"Just tell him, brother." Pugliese's voice was hollow. "I've seen what this man can do firsthand." Her expression was downcast and defeated. "He is a butcher. A madman. He slayed every last man at the estate. All of Salvo's men. Every one of them." She glared at Bishop with her remaining eye. "Do not expect mercy from this man, he has none."

Suddenly animated, Dario stared daggers at his sibling. "What the fuck do I care what you think, woman? You have no face left. You're hideous. Who will fuck you now, huh? No one. Even the dogs wouldn't go near your filthy puttana figa now."

With great pleasure, Bishop punched the mafia boss in the stomach. He doubled over and retched.

"Now, now," Bishop took a step back to keep his shoes vomit-free, "let's not say anything we'll regret at the Christmas table this year, shall we?" Circling around Dario, he grabbed a chunk of his jet-black hair and yanked it back. "I'm steadily losing patience, and you're running out of time." Bishop screamed into the vomit-flecked face before him. "Where is Yousef Sharif?"

Bishop finally witnessed Dario's complete fear. It had taken less time than anticipated, but there it was. The Italian covered it as soon as it appeared, but it was too late. Bishop had seen it. He'd broken through. Now all he had to do was finish the job and they would have Sharif's location.

Rolling up his sleeves, Bishop went to work.

Over the next hour, he broke Dario Pugliese thoroughly. Using every technique he possessed, Bishop shattered every defence the man had until the barricades crumbled and he stood alone, naked and afraid. He would tell his captor anything to make it stop. And he did. Not only did Bishop extract the location of the troublesome Saudi prince, he also obtained the number of guards and their level of training, their security set-up, weapons, everything.

Dario Pugliese was no fool. The precautions he'd taken and his choice of fortifications to protect his newly acquired trophy were formidable. Fifteen highly trained mafia mercenaries and a literal fortress stood between Bishop's team and Yousef Sharif. Not only that, there would also be Istanbul itself to deal with if they succeeded in their first stage. It was still a city on edge; likely even worse now, after a shootout at one of its most popular parks and foreigners murdered in broad daylight. It was obvious something was about to break, but no one was quite sure what.

Bishop didn't know if Oleg was done with the whole endeavour. It would be wishful thinking to believe he'd given up his personal vendetta against Astrid and returned to Mother Russia to join a knitting commune, or whatever it was he did when he wasn't being an enormous pain in the arse.

Add to all that, Astrid was still out there, somewhere. Her team had been killed by Dario's men, her prize stolen from her grasp. She would be seeking vengeance. Bishop knew she would tear the city apart to get back what she'd lost. There was only one thing on the planet more dangerous than Astrid Spencer, and that was an angry, vengeful Astrid Spencer. No one in the city would be safe from her wrath.

One thing was for certain; the mission was nowhere near over. As Bishop and his team checked over their weapons, he knew it had only just begun.

# CHAPTER ELEVEN

"Eyes on the patrol. We have a new one. Ooh, he's a big bugger. It's like someone strapped an Uzi to an over-stuffed bag of oranges. He probably gets his steroids in bulk. Hah, bulk. I'm hilarious."

"No need for the running commentary, thank you."

Bishop tried to keep Fitzherbert's extraneous comments on the guards patrolling Dario's fortress to a minimum. While her surveillance was critical to the mission, her humour was a distraction they could do without. He suspected it was her way of dealing with Lanaway's death. While Bishop understood that the grieving process varied for everyone, they had a time-critical mission and needed no further diversions.

"Understood, boss. The guard's done a sweep and headed back into the East entrance, exactly like the others. Ten minutes on the button. It's as if these guys want to be picked off."

She was right. Any well-trained soldier knew to keep their patrol timing uneven. Setting regimented patterns begged for reprisal. And Bishop and his team were just the ones to deliver it.

The old fortress Dario had hired stood on a hill high above the Golden Horn, a horn-shaped estuary that was the primary inlet on the Bosporus. The traffic on the river was bustling with commercial and sight-seeing vessels. Further down the river were conference centres and tourist parks. The target itself was a high-walled stronghold dating back to the late 1800s, built for a garrison situated on the river to hold off a Russian invasion. Back then the small fortress would have done little to stop an entire Russian army had it arrived, but the high red-brick walls were enough to slow down a small modern incursion. It was an added headache to an already complicated assignment.

It wasn't the only one.

"Any other… activity around the compound?" Bishop's team knew what he meant. Any sign of Astrid.

"No. No sign." Bridgeman's normally neutral tone carried a hint of disdain. "Are our orders still the same if… the activity is spotted, sir?"

Bishop chose his words carefully. "Yes. Alert the team, but do not illuminate the target. The target's worth more alive."

"But sir…" Fitzherbert did her best to remain neutral. Unlike Bridgeman, she didn't remotely succeed. "I… I'm not questioning the orders, but are you *sure* that's tactically the best course of action?"

It was clear neither of his team agreed that they should hold back if they had Lanaway's murderer in their sights. Regardless, Bishop knew they would follow his command. As much as they'd want to put a bullet through Astrid's skull, they'd do as instructed.

"Affirmative. We take her alive if we can." He swallowed. "She has a lot of intelligence on a vast criminal network. It's our only chance to bring it down from the inside. If circumstances change, you'll be the first to know."

"Understood."

"Understood."

Bishop was sure they didn't. It was a topic for another time. First they had to rescue the troublesome Yousef Sharif, whether he liked it or not. There was a part of Bishop that hoped they would raid the compound, extract their quarry and be out of Turkey before they caught sight of Astrid. He knew it was wishful thinking, though. The woman had a way of re-entering his life in the most dramatic and violent fashion possible.

Bishop had to focus. There was only one target on this mission: the head of the OPEC Board of Governors and the next in line to the throne of the second-largest oil producer on the planet. He had to extract him in time for the OPEC vote or the world would tumble into economic turmoil. Squeezing his binoculars tight, Bishop tried to remind himself of that. He almost succeeded.

Positioned in an abandoned luxury apartment across the road from the old fortress, Bishop covered the front entrance. Turreted guard towers loomed over two imposing wooden gates. To the left, Bishop could see Bridgeman's position, high in the cabin of a crane over-looking the compound. It had cost them several thousand lira to bribe the construction crew to take the afternoon off. Fitzherbert covered the rear of the building. A recent modification had knocked down a large portion of the rear wall, which had been replaced by a cyclone wire fence, somewhat defeating the purpose of a fortress. All three counted down the minutes until their agreed go-time.

Despite the limited window, the plan had still been meticulously crafted, down to the finest detail. Thankfully, the fortress had well documented structural plans freely available on the internet. All three members of the team had specific roles, with the most precise timings. There was minimal margin of error. Bridgeman, in particular, had emerged as a master strategist. The plan was like a Swiss watch.

Bishop slowed his breathing, walking through every scenario in his mind. He anticipated his team's reactions, their strengths, their weaknesses, what they would require of him in a myriad of situations. They were ready.

"Uh, boss?" Bridgeman's voice was taught. "You know that thing you wanted to keep an eye out for? It's… at the front gate."

Bishop sighed and looked at his watch. "Of course she is."

With a grunt, Bishop raised himself up, tucked his pistol into his shoulder holster and threw on his jacket. *This woman.*

Stepping into the bright sunshine, Bishop shielded his eyes and waited for them to adjust. Bridgeman was right. Fifty metres in front of the great wooden gate stood a figure. And what a figure. Astrid stood, legs akimbo, in combat boots and a sundress that hugged her curves. She also carried something on her shoulder.

Bishop slowly stepped towards her. She didn't turn.

"Hey, Astrid." Bishop used his friendliest voice. "Where'd you get the grenade launcher?"

She pointed to her face. "Arms dealer." She smiled without turning, seemingly amusing herself.

"Oh, yeah. Right."

Her eyes were wild. Wilder than he'd ever seen, Bishop thought at first, but it was a lie. He'd seen them just as wild several times before. When he'd been strapped to a torturer's slab and she held a scalpel in her hand, while lunging at him on a boat suspended by a crane, in the throes of passion. That kind of thing. Bishop had seen wildness in Astrid Spencer's eyes on many occasions.

"Whatcha doing here, Astrid?"

She shrugged, and the launcher bobbed up and down on her shoulder. "Just taking in the sights."

"That's some awfully big weaponry you have there."

Astrid gave him a slanted grin. "I could say the exact same thing to you, my love."

"I meant the grenade launcher."

"Oh, right. Don't you read the tourist warnings? The streets of Istanbul aren't safe for single women. Just a little precaution."

"Wouldn't you say that's overkill?"

"Have you met me?" She chuckled. "When do I ever do things by halves?"

"You can't storm a fortress in a sundress and combat boots."

"Watch me." Her expression turned stony. "Those fuckers killed my team. People who were as close to family as you can be in this business. They're going to pay."

The grenade launcher and her sunny casual attire added to the unhinged impression. Astrid's usual persona was unpredictable with a hint of megalomania, but even then, she always carried a sense of control. While her actions may have been erratic, they were always focused on an end she had perfect command of. Now, that command was gone. She was frayed, and appeared to be acting on impulse with no restraint. That was a truly terrifying thought.

Astrid grunted. "I'm going to make Dario pay for what he did to my people. He slaughtered them, all of them. I'm getting back what's rightfully mine."

"Dario and his sister are halfway to England by now.

As for what's rightfully yours, I think we'll need to agree to disagree."

The fire in her eyes was directed at him now. "You won't stop me, Bishop."

"I beg to differ, I'm afraid."

A bright red dot appeared in the centre of her yellow dress. Bishop nodded to the sniper's nest high on the crane.

Astrid looked up, mouth open in shock. "You'd take me out?"

"If I recall correctly," Bishop frowned, "you said I'd take you out one way or another."

She frowned. "It was funny when I said it." Astrid's attention returned the great wooden gates. "You could've killed me so many times over, but you didn't. You won't now."

"Situation's changed, Astrid. We're not under fire now. You murdered an MI6 agent. I can't let that go. I offered you a chance to come in and face the consequences of what you've done, and afterwards we could have seen where you and I were. That was your one chance. You didn't take it. Don't think you have a free pass here. You need to stand down. We're taking you in."

She turned to him, her eyes moist. There was genuine shock in her expression. Astrid looked at him as if for the last time, then put her eye to the launcher's optical sight.

"Think this through, Astrid. You can't take on a squad of mercenaries singlehandedly."

Her face was harder now. "I built the largest illegal arms-dealing organisation the world has ever seen *single-handedly*, I can take down these clowns."

"No, Astrid, you can't. It's over. Your team is gone, this is an official MI6 operation now. More agents are on the way." Bishop checked his watch. "In about two minutes a mercenary will be patrolling the parapet, spot you and start firing. You can either come with me or die in the street. Your choice."

"There's a third option."

Astrid pulled the trigger. Smoke trailed from the grenade launcher as the missile snaked its way to the target, then the ancient wooden doors exploded into splinters and smoke. Fragments of wood and masonry flew in all directions. The surrounding neighbourhood descended into chaos. Men and women screamed, dogs barked, sirens screeched.

Bishop hit his comms. "Plan Omega. Go!"

Over the comms, Bridgeman huffed, which Bishop took to mean he was scaling down the crane mast. "Oh good, we're doing the balls-to-wall, last-resort plan. Brilliant."

Bishop ignored the jibe. "We go, now!"

"I thought you'd never ask." Astrid grinned and crouched, ready to sprint. "Last one to Sharif drops their pants."

"Not this time, I'm afraid."

From his pocket, Bishop extracted a midget syringe, a gadget from MI6's boffins that he'd selected from the weapons pack supplied for the mission. Shorter and far more potent than its hospital-issued counterpart, 'The Midge' packed a punch and then some. Inserted into the vertebral vein of Astrid's neck, it performed its job in seconds.

First Astrid's eyes glazed over. Next her limbs failed her. The grenade launcher clattered to the ground, her spaghetti arms no longer able to hold it. Her head lazily swivelled to Bishop, her relaxed face etched with confusion.

With a swollen tongue, she slurred. "How… how did you do that?"

Bishop pointed to his face. "Spy."

Astrid collapsed and Bishop caught her. Scooping her up, Bishop threw her over his shoulder and fireman carried her to his former position in the abandoned apartment. He laid her out on the couch in the front room. She'd be out for a good five or six hours, given her body mass, perhaps more. Bishop locked the door and broke into a run.

He had a fortress to storm.

The front of the stronghold was a wreck. The smouldering ruins of the once-great wooden gate lay between collapsed red brick walls.

The moment Bishop reached the decimated front gates, Bridgeman strode silently and confidently up to his superior. Various armaments were lashed to the big man. He looked like a GI Joe action figure brought to life.

"You have enough weaponry there, slick?"

Bridgeman didn't move a muscle. "Yep. Even have a little Double Tap derringer strapped to my ankle if all else fails."

Bishop nodded. "Want to kill some mafia bad guys?"

"And it's not even my birthday." He cocked his SA80 carbine rifle. "On three?"

Bishop unslung his carbine and began counting. "Three—"

"Excuse me, boss."

Bridgeman placed his hand gently on Bishop's shoulder, causing him to stop his count. Before Bishop could ask why, the big man fired one round into the still-swirling smoke of the fortress. There was a brief cry and then out of the haze a khaki-clad mercenary fell forward, a red hole in the centre of his forehead.

Casually lifting an eyebrow, Bridgeman addressed the fallen man. "That 5.56 mm round was courtesy of His Majesty's government. If you liked your death, please consider leaving a review on our Facebook page. Thank you, and have a nice day."

Bishop manoeuvred his rifle around in search of further threats. None immediately showed. "You're a mad bastard, aren't you?"

Bridgeman grinned. "Yes, sir, I believe I am."

"Good lad." Bishop hit comms. "You in position, Team Haggis?"

"I love a good position, me, Team Posh." Fitzherbert was chipper, considering the bullets had started to fly. "Ready for the load."

Bishop gave the slightest shake of his head. "Phrasing."

"Oh, right, sorry, Team Posh." A metallic snapping of switches sounded over the comms. "Open your mouths boys, I'm gonna blow."

Before Bishop could chastise his subordinate, the explosions sounded. At the rear of the fortress four successive blasts echoed throughout the neighbourhood. It wasn't what Bishop had planned, but it would do.

With a nod to each other, Bridgeman and Bishop sprinted into the breach and took cover behind a Ford sedan parked in the middle of the courtyard. From the main building two mafia mercenaries threw open a door and spilled into the compound, seeking targets. They were too slow. Each MI6 man fired once, and both mercenaries fell before they'd even laid eyes on their targets.

Their cohorts seemed a little wiser. Instead of recklessly running into an unknown fray, they hid behind the brick wall, poked their AK-308s out the door and fired blindly. Not exactly a surgical strike, but it was a safer option. Or so they thought.

If Bishop recalled his high school physics correctly, force equals mass times acceleration. Any projectile could theoretically penetrate another, it just needed the right conditions. He unslung his Colt Carbine C8, which was loaded with heavy steel core rounds. Bishop had the right conditions.

Firing twice, Bishop blew soccer ball-sized holes in the brickwork on either side of the open door. The assault rifles which had been firing a frenzy of bullets fell to the ground, no longer attached to live combatants.

In the space of a minute they had decimated Dario's forces by a third. Bishop knew it only got harder from here. The element of surprise was lost; any half-decent soldier would be shaking off the shock and reassessing the battleground. They would regroup and hunker down. Now shit got real.

"Boss, eleven o'clock high."

Bridgeman pointed up. Bishop was right, the enemy was reassessing the battleground. A drone moved into the air, no doubt attempting to gather an assessment of the combat zone. Perhaps they weren't as inept as first impressions had suggested.

The drone was a shrewd move, an essential part of modern warfare. Have eyes on the terrain and your enemy one step ahead. Bishop couldn't allow that.

He hit comms. "Team Haggis, we have eyes in the sky."

"Roger that, Posh." Fitzherbert's voice was strained, as though she was reaching for something. "On it."

Indeed she was. Almost the exact instant she had completed her sentence, another aerial vehicle flew into view. Nicknamed *The Elmer*, the automated anti-drone drone flew from Fitzherbert's position at the rear of the fortress, directly towards the other drone. The Elmer performed its role perfectly, zeroing in on the enemy drone. When it was within ten metres, Elmer shot out a gimballed netgun, ensnaring the smaller drone on a tethered steel cable. Elmer flew away with the other drone in its net, leaving the mafia mercenaries not only with no intelligence, but with the knowledge that they were thoroughly outclassed.

Bishop tapped comms again. "Haggis, ready for maelstrom fire in five."

"Roger that, Posh."

Five seconds later, Fitzherbert delivered once more. The sound of multiple remote-operated machine guns spurted forth and a flurry of fire echoed around the fortress. Fitzherbert had rigged the guns to spray the rear of the fortress in an arc, left to right, appearing as though multiple assailants were firing at once. It may have been a diversion, but it sounded like a small invasion.

At the front of the compound, Bishop pointed towards the door he had just decimated, indicating to Bridgeman that they should storm it now that they had their distraction.

"Fuck!" Fitzherbert let out a cry of surprise. "Sorry for the language, Posh, but some douchestick just ran out a rear entrance like this is Butch Cassidy and the Sundance Kid. He survived like it is, too. Oh, crap! Another guy just did the same. Two more down. Who trained these guys, Ray fucken' Charles?"

That was eight down by Bishop's count. There were apparently fifteen in the compound. The odds were improving, but nothing could be taken for granted. At the rear of the building, Bishop heard one of the automated guns stop, then another. They were running out of ammunition. Their decoy attack would lose effectiveness in seconds.

"We're advancing now."

"Roger that, Posh. Keep your tooshies safe, boys."

Bishop and Bridgeman dashed from the cover of the Ford across the open courtyard. No one fired at them. At the rear of the complex the maelstrom of auto-fire ceased entirely, their diversion at an end. The two MI6 men leapt through the front entrance.

The hallway was dark; the only light came from the holes Bishop had blasted. The product of those shots lay on the poorly lit floor: two mercenaries, one with half a head missing, the other with a bloodied chest that drew no breath.

The two men covered opposite ends of the hall. No combatant aimed a weapon at them. In fact, no sound could be heard at all. Bishop was experienced enough not to take it as a good sign. He stabbed two fingers towards the end of the hall, which led to the main section of the ancient fortress. They stepped forward cautiously, weapons raised, fingers on triggers.

"Heads up, Posh. Local police have been alerted. Units incoming. ETA five minutes. Do your thing, but faster."

Bishop replied quietly. "Acknowledged."

The two MI6 agents slowly stalked down the hallway, ready for any sort of attack. But none came. No shots fired. No sound could be heard at all. The lack of confrontation put Bishop even more on edge.

Reaching the end of the darkened hall, they halted. Bishop gave Bridgeman a nod. The other man lowered his weapon and reached for the array slung on his back.

Bridgeman pulled the pin on the grenade. "This is for all those Turkish Delights."

Bishop smirked. "Racist much?"

Bridgeman threw the grenade through the doorway. "I'd do the same for Bounty. Who the fuck puts coconut in a chocolate bar?"

The explosion silenced any reply Bishop might have given. The two men stormed through the gap, weapons at the ready. The room was full of swirling smoke and charred debris, but there was no one there. Gun barrels scanned for targets, but there were none.

"I don't like this." For the first time, Bridgeman's voice held an edge.

Bishop nodded, and jerked his head towards the only door left. His counterpart acknowledged the order. The worn wooden door looked solid. Bridgeman unslung his shotgun and pointed to the hinges. Bishop nodded and held his carbine at the ready. With two precise breaching shotgun blasts, Bridgeman destroyed the hinges. The door fell away and the two men leapt into the next room.

Amid the darkness and swirling smoke, the vast room held little and everything, all at once. In the centre of the bare brick room were two figures. Sitting shackled to a rickety wooden chair sat one very frightened and bruised looking Yousef Sharif. His cheeks were hollow and there were black circles around his glazed eyes. He was malnourished and glassy-eyed, but alive. The other figure in the room didn't seem much better off.

He had a shaved head and wore the same khaki attire of the other mercenaries, but he was so thin the uniform hung off him like a tent. In his shaking hand he held what appeared to be a Nazi-era Luger. He couldn't have been over eighteen. Not exactly in keeping with the crack military outfit Dario had alluded to. The poor kid was the last line of defence.

Holstering his pistol, Bishop approached with his palms held high. Bridgeman made no such move. He had the kid well and truly in his sights.

Shouting across the void between them, Bishop tried his best rudimentary Turkish. "Do you speak English?"

The kid nodded. "A little." It was heavily accented, but passable.

Bishop gave him a nod by way of thanks. "We're taking him now." It was a statement, not a question. "I suggest you walk away and never look back. It is an offer your comrades did not receive. Do you understand?"

It took a few moments for the words to translate, then the young kid's face morphed from panic to the faintest glimmer of hope. "You... I can go?"

Bishop nodded.

"No...?" He made a gun with his fingers—a redundant move, given that he already held one—and made a *boom* sound.

"Correct, no..." Bishop mimicked the gesture and sound.

The kid didn't have to be told twice. He dropped the ancient Luger and bolted. Every step of the way, Bridgeman had him in his sights. After he'd left the room, the big man kept aiming at the door. After twenty seconds, when he was sure the kid had actually left, Bridgeman turned.

"What now, boss?"

"Already on it."

Indeed, he was. Bishop pulled out his set of handcuff skeleton keys. The third worked like a charm. He freed Sharif, who warily rubbed his wrists.

"Time to go, Your Highness." Bishop helped him to his feet.

"Where... where are *you* from?" A natural question for a victim of multiple kidnappings. His expression was a mixture of trepidation, fear and wariness.

"MI6, Your Highness. We're here to get you home."

"Home?" He blinked several times. "I would very much like to see my home."

"I'm sure." Bishop paused. He didn't feel comfortable asking the next question, but it needed to be asked. "Your Highness, during your incarceration, here and the previous one, did you, ah, did you happen to engage in activities that may not play well at home?" On receiving a blank look, Bishop went on. "In my culture, same-sex activities are neither illegal nor frowned upon, but if there is footage of you engaging in—"

"That question is pure impertinence!" It seemed there was still some spark left in the prince.

"Yes, I imagine it is, but I'm asking anyway. If there's video of you in a compromising position, don't you think it's best we grab it now?"

"There is no such thing, I assure you!"

"You're sure? Last chance."

"The former, and far more civilised, captors tried to tempt me, but it was an obvious ruse. I remained chaste."

Bishop shrugged. "Fine."

Either Astrid's plan had failed or it had been interrupted by Dario's goons before it could play out. Either way, Bishop had to get Sharif out of Istanbul and back to Saudi Arabia before the OPEC vote.

"Let's get you home, Your Highness." As politely as he could, Bishop pushed the prince back the way they had come. "Right now, we need to get as far away from here as possible."

The three walked as fast as Sharif's weakened legs could carry him. Bridgeman remained vigilant for any threats.

"And then what?" Sharif became more animated. "What is to become of me when I return home?"

Bishop's body suddenly felt a million years old. It was no longer fuelled by adrenaline. He was exhausted, beaten down and utterly depleted. It took all his concentration to keep putting one foot in front of the other.

"Your Highness, I say this with the utmost respect." Bishop checked the hallway before gently guiding Sharif forward. "I honestly don't give a shit." He ignored the prince's expression of shock mixed with self-important disdain. "Too many people have died because of you;

you don't get to feel hard done by. You need to understand we're not saving you, we're saving the world from what it would become if you fell into the wrong hands. It's as simple as that."

The three trod down the hallway towards the two bodies near the front door. Bishop took the lead, Bridgeman stayed beside the prince.

"If it helps, Your Highness," Bridgeman leaned over and spoke quietly, "I don't give a shit either." He smiled sweetly. "Just so we're all on the same page."

Yousef Sharif was too shocked to talk. Bishop cast his teammate a sideways smirk.

He contacted Fitzherbert to advise they were on their way and she should pack up and bug out. "I'm already in a pub in Edenborough, twats," she responded.

All three men slowed as they reached the brightly lit front entrance. No longer fatigued, Bishop, like Bridgeman, was back in the game. The big man motioned with his fingers that he'd take a gander through the hole punched through the red brickwork by Bishop's previous blast.

Poking his head into the gap, it took all of two seconds for Bridgeman's expression to turn grave. "We have a problem."

Bishop frowned. "Reinforcements?"

"Not quite." He jerked his head for Bishop to have a look.

His superior did exactly that. Bishop immediately understood Bridgeman's trepidation. The entire splintered entrance to the ancient fortress was swarming with police. Their flashing lights bounced off the fortified walls; any chance of escape was blocked. They'd missed their window by seconds.

"We could fight our way through..." Bridgeman raised his weapon.

"Stand down, soldier. These are the good guys." Bishop shook his head. "Taking down mafia mercenaries who take blood money is one thing, shooting innocent police who are performing their duty is another."

Bridgeman seemed relieved. "What do you suggest?"

Bishop hit comms. "Change of plans, Haggis. We're headed your way. ETA ninety seconds."

Bridgeman shoved Sharif, forcing him to join them in a trot in the direction they'd come from.

"The hell?" Fitzherbert breathed heavily as if she was jogging herself. "I just fookin' bugged out."

"The cops at the entrance are terribly sorry to inconvenience you."

"Fuckers." There was a thump, as if she'd dropped down. "Rear entrance clear. But make it fast, I can't guarantee it's going to stay that way. Burn some rubber, boys."

"On it."

Bursting through the rear entrance two things hit Bishop at once. The bright sunshine quickly gave way to the scene of absolute carnage. Fitzherbert's automated gunfire had pockmarked the entire rear of the fortress, including the two unfortunate souls who'd been fool enough to storm out among it. Their bodies lay bloodied and roasting in the sun.

The three had no time no pay them any heed. Sprinting towards the gate in the cyclone fence, Bishop held his gun by his side. He had no wish to shoot any police, but if it meant not spending the rest of his life in a Turkish prison, he would certainly wing a few.

Thankfully, no one needed to be shot. They met no opposition. The three raced across the road and around the corner to find a harangued Fitzherbert waiting for them beside their getaway Range Rover.

Bishop nodded behind him. "You don't do things by halves, do you?"

"You should see me on a dance floor." Fitzherbert grinned. "Take no bloody prisoners, me."

Bishop gave an exhausted smile as the three MI6 agents piled into the SUV. Sharif remained standing on the sidewalk.

He crossed his arms. "Why should I go with you people?"

Fitzherbert grunted in disbelief. "Because we saved your royal arse."

"I do not know who you are! I do not want to go with you. I can make it on my own."

In the backseat, Bridgeman mumbled, "Ungrateful son of a bitch."

"You're right, Sharif, of course." Bishop's words were weary. He glanced up and down the deserted street. "But there are at least three other factions in this city who want to kidnap you, and they won't treat you anywhere near as politely as we have. Add to that, you'll make it about five metres before the police pick you up and charge you with every crime ever invented. And that's if the assassins don't get you first." Bishop put on his seatbelt. "The choice is completely yours, of course."

Bishop started the Range Rover. Without a word, Sharif opened the back door and slunk into his seat. His eyes were downcast as he put on his seatbelt.

In the front seat, Fitzherbert shook her head. "Dickhead."

Sharif's head snapped up. "You are addressing His Royal Highness. Show some respect!"

Fitzherbert groaned and grabbed her crotch. "Respect this. You know how many people died because of you? You get respect when you avoid the cluster-fuck those twats who kidnapped you tried to create, alright? Until then…" She grabbed her crotch again for emphasis.

Bridgeman clapped his hands together. "Next stop, the Lamb and Flag on Covent Garden. First round's on His Royal High-pants."

Bishop put the car into gear and took off. "We need to make one stop first."

The Range Rover cruised the neighbourhood for half an hour before Bishop felt safe enough to park. The sun was setting, and life had returned to the streets. With it came a lot of spectators, curious to see what had occurred at the old fortress. Nothing attracted a crowd quite like a crowd, and the police cordon was loaded with rubber-neckers. Several chanted anti-government slogans, as if it were all their government's fault.

Pulling up to a free spot, Bishop put the Range Rover in park and cut the engine. All three passengers were clearly unimpressed.

"I'll just be a minute."

He received no response. Not that he expected any.

Crossing the sidewalk, he unlocked the door to the abandoned luxury apartment where he'd stashed Astrid. He understood why Sharif would be hesitant to collect the woman responsible for his initial incarceration. Equally, he knew why Bridgeman and Fitzherbert thought him insane: the woman had killed their former team leader. This woman was responsible for everything.

The door opened with a *creak*. It took a moment for Bishop's eyes to adjust to the darkened interior. Every-thing was how he'd left it—almost. There was only one thing missing.

Astrid. The couch she had laid on was bare, although

something had been left in her place. How had she recovered so soon? The dose he'd given her would have felled a linebacker for five hours. It didn't make sense.

With pistol drawn, Bishop approached the couch cautiously, scanning the room for any sign of life. There didn't appear to be any. He leant down and retrieved the note. The hand-scrawled message contained only a few words.

*I told you this was not over, Englishman.*

# CHAPTER TWELVE

"You what, boss?"

The expression of bewilderment on his two subordinates' faces was exactly what Bishop had expected. Even before he'd said the words, he knew they wouldn't understand. Hell, he barely did. It was complete madness and all three of them knew it.

They'd gone straight to the airport, where a chartered plane was being fuelled for their flight to London. All three stood in the small departure lounge used by movie stars and the stupefyingly rich. It was empty except for the three MI6 agents.

Sharif was already onboard, sedated and on a saline drip. The British government was taking no chances, and ensured he wouldn't remain in the country a second longer than necessary. Not only were several hostile factions potentially still prowling the city, but the city itself was set to explode.

The opposition party had blamed the government for the murders at Sultanahmet Square and Dario's fortress. The already unpopular government had denied any involvement, which only fuelled suspicions. The opposition called the deaths politically motivated assassinations, and demanded that the entire government be sacked.

It was all the spark the city needed. Rioting erupted in at least three neighbourhoods. The governor called a state of emergency and instigated a curfew. There were rumours roadblocks would be erected within hours. All foreigners were ordered to stay in their hotels. The main airport had been shut down after rioters had driven flaming lorries onto the main runway. The private MI6 flight would be the last out of the city. Istanbul was about to detonate, and his organisation wanted Bishop and his team far from it when it did.

Which made Bishop's decision all the more insane.

Fitzherbert shook her head in disbelief. "You want to go back there. Alone? For her?"

"Not *for* her, no." Bishop spoke slowly, trying to be as clear as possible. "Well, not like that, anyway." Bishop felt flushed. "She's a wanted felon. She murdered a member of MI6, she needs to be extradited to face those charges in the UK. She needs to face justice."

"She's going to face justice." Bridgeman's face was stern. "The Russians already have her. That's justice enough in my book."

Bishop spoke as emotionlessly as he could. "She has information that will assist His Majesty's government, about Kali, about a great many things."

"And just what are you going to do if you find her?" Bridgeman spoke for the first time in a while. "Your team's leaving in ten minutes. Your mission is done."

Fitzherbert placed her hand on Bridgeman's forearm. "Drop it, yeah?" She turned to Bishop. "He's going no matter what. I think he needs to do this."

Bishop gave her a grateful smile. "Thank you."

"Don't thank me, you wanker." She shook her head.

"You're the one who'll have to face the brass when this is done." She gave him a weak grin. "Go do what you have to. Try not to get killed."

"That's sweet. You care."

"No, I bloody do not." She planted her fists on her hips "And you're buying the first five rounds when you get your sorry arse back to London."

Bishop gave her a nod. "That's a deal."

"Too bloody right it is."

Bridgeman rocked on his heels. "You need us to cover for you, boss?"

Bishop was surprised by that the offer. Despite knowing that Bishop was risking his career to track down the woman who had murdered Lanaway, Bridgeman was willing to lie to MI6 for him. The significance of the offer was not lost on him.

"Thank you for offering, but this is my choice. I'll bear the consequences. This is on me alone. Report only the truth."

The big man leaned down, unstrapped his ankle holster and tossed it to Bishop. "Take the derringer, just in case."

Accepting it, Bishop patted him on the shoulder. Fitzherbert rolled her eyes.

"Gawd, get a room, you two. This man has places to be. Now go!"

And go he did. Bishop sprinted out of the terminal and made a phone call. It was answered on the second ring.

"So, you are not dead?"

Bishop couldn't help but smile. "Not yet. I have a small favour."

It took only moments for Bishop to tell Demir what he needed. It was four times as long before his friend was able to reply.

"I admit, this is not what I expected you to ask. This is not a small favour, my friend."

Bishop knew that already. "Can you do it?" He held his breath.

"It seems to me," it sounded like Demir was choosing his words carefully, "that you are more than happy to come and say hello or call me on the telephone when you want something. And yet, when I provide information, you do not take it seriously, and even worse, do not even handle the mission yourself until it is too late. No, my friend, I believe we are not equals here. What is the American phrase? This is a one-way street, yes?"

Not all of what he said was true. He had taken Demir's information seriously; it had only been Astrid's interreference that took him away from the mission. But a lot of it was.

Only partially joking, Bishop asked, "Do you want me to marry one of your daughters?"

"Don't make me kill you, Bishop. That is a terrible thing to contemplate!" He let out a good-natured chuckle. "Oh my, could you imagine? I hate to think where that thing of yours has been. No matter how they try my patience, I would never submit them to such a repugnant thought!"

"I don't know how to respond to that."

Demir sighed. "Perhaps you could begin by telling me the Russian's name, and any aliases."

The streets of Istanbul were aflame. Literally.

On the journey into the heart of the city, Bishop's taxi passed three burning cars, as well as hordes of protesters in makeshift disguises. Through glimpses down side streets, Bishop observed throngs massing, carrying signs, chunks of wood and angry dispositions.

The driver didn't speak English, except for his oft-repeated, "No good. No good."

When they braked to let through a group of chanting protesters, the driver turned to Bishop and mimed stopping the car, running, and then made a triangle over his head. His meaning was clear: when he'd dropped Bishop off he was going home. The streets were far too dangerous.

Bishop wasn't about to disagree with him.

A troop carrier hurtled down the street in the opposite direction, the sides of the truck blackened. The damage appeared fresh. A Molotov cocktail? Bishop caught only the briefest glimpse of the three faces in the front cabin. Every one of the young soldiers looked panicked.

Only a madman would be heading into the chaos of the city now.

Demir had come through, just as Bishop knew he would. Through 'sources', he had heard through a 'friend of a friend' that a group of Russians had hired the penthouse suite on the top floor of the Doruk Palas Hotel, a small luxury hotel in the centre of Istanbul. They had apparently bribed a touring Australian pop band to vacate the suite in exchange for a promise of visas for a future Russian tour. The gay lead singer had previously been refused a visa on the grounds of being a disruptive influence on Russia's youth. Bishop should have been surprised at the level of detail Demir had accumulated in such a short amount of time. He wasn't.

The phrasing Demir had used disturbed Bishop. He'd distinctly used the words 'group of Russians'. As large as he was, Oleg wasn't a group. His appearance at Sultanahmet Square had been a solo effort. If he had a team, like Bishop, he should have covered the area with members at strategic points, but he hadn't.

What gave the story more credibility was the detail about a Russian carrying a 'drunk blonde girl' to the suite. Bishop had not told Demir about Astrid, only that he was looking for Oleg. It was that point which propelled him to act.

When the taxi pulled up a block short of the hotel, Bishop handed a wad of notes to the driver. In return, he took off before Bishop had fully shut the door. The streets were deserted, bar the occasional hooded figure who scurried in the shadows.

Taking in the eight-storey hotel, Bishop considered his options. Walking through the front door would be fraught with danger. If Oleg did indeed have a team, then Bishop couldn't take the risk. He had to choose a more subtle means of ingress.

Circling around the back of the building, Bishop hung in the half-light across from the service entry. The roller door was up, revealing a truck bay and several access doors. Each had a keypad, indicating a semblance of security. Given the right equipment, Bishop could force his way in, either violently or through technology. But he didn't have those tools with him, just his pistol, Bridgeman's two-shot derringer and some spare ammunition. He'd need another entry method. He'd try capitalism.

On the street outside the service entrance a porter stood alone, smoking a cigarette. Bishop crossed the street and offered the smoker a friendly wave. He mimed smoking a cigarette, and pointed to the man's hand. Shoulders sloping with a groan, the porter took out a soft pack of Camels from his top pocket and shook one to the top. Bishop extracted a cigarette and accepted the proffered light. Inhaling, he gave a nod of thanks. The bumming a smoke ritual was the same the world over.

Doing his best not to choke on the noxious cylinder, Bishop reached into his pocket and extracted a large roll of lira. He peeled off a handful and handed them to the startled porter. It was roughly the equivalent of a week's wage. The porter's eyes were like plates.

Bishop smiled.

The top floor of the Doruk Palas hotel was ominously quiet. Only one hotel room occupied the entire floor: the penthouse suite. There was no sound from a TV, nor the sound of a shower or any human activity. No light shone from under the door and no trays sat outside the room. For all intents and purposes, it appeared deserted. But it wasn't.

The tripwire Bishop spotted by the stair entrance told him Demir's intelligence was on the money. He slunk down the short hallway, gun drawn, sticking to the wall-papered wall. The entrance to the penthouse suite was a grandiose set of double doors.

Gun in his right hand, doorknob in his left, Bishop turned the handle and listened intently. There was no sound. The door was unlocked, which only put him more on edge. He flung the grand doors open and dove to the right, rolling to the corner of the room, gun ready to unleash hell. Only, he didn't need to.

There were no targets. No one fired. Bishop was alone.

The dark hotel room seemed undisturbed. The only noteworthy feature was an iPad propped up in the centre of the dining table. Taped to the front was a hand-scrawled note in the same handwriting Bishop had seen earlier. It contained only two words.

*Play me.*

Hand hovering over the screen, Bishop hesitated. Knowing the man behind the message, it could have been a trap. In fact, it likely was. Bishop unlocked the screen and pressed play anyway.

"What kind of idiot spy are you?" Oleg's ghostly face asked on screen. The light was low, but the footage had certainly been taken in the room were Bishop now stood; the furniture matched exactly. On the screen, Oleg shook his head. "I mean, you see a sign that says 'play me' and don't suppose it is attached to explosives, eh? You are far too trusting." He paused, his face contemplative. "But I suppose I am too, da? I trusted we were on the same side, that you wanted to bring the evil witch down as much as I did." He lowered his gaze. "But I was wrong, wasn't I, Englishman? You were protecting her. Even now, you come to her rescue like a swashbuckler man from the old movies." Oleg frowned and then shrugged. "You are too late. She is dead. Hers is just another body that will wash up in the Black Sea at some point, causing headlines for a day or two and then soon forgotten." His sinister grin was pure malevolence. "But not by you, Bishop, hmmm? You and I will hopefully meet again some day. Now that we know each other's true nature, it will be an interesting meeting, I think. Goodbye, Englishman." He paused. "Oh, and bribing staff to sneak into a hotel? Such a cliché. You are a poor excuse for a spy. There, I said it. This device will self-destruct in five seconds. Five. Four. Three. Two. One." Oleg chuckled. "Self-destruct? You probably did a dive roll or something. Idiot."

Oleg's hand moved forward to end the recording, and then he was gone. The black screen reflected Bishop's worn face back at him. Astrid was dead.

Astrid.

Dead.

Bishop tried to let the words sink in, but they

wouldn't. Like rain falling on an umbrella, they couldn't penetrate. Bishop knew he should feel something, but all he felt was numb. Denial was a powerful reflex.

Staring at the iPad, he fumed. He'd been played thoroughly, again. Oleg knew Bishop bribed a porter to gain access, so he must have been at the hotel. Probably. It could also be that Oleg knew him so well he'd predicted his actions.

Bishop replayed the video. The second viewing garnered a detail he'd missed the first time. Over Oleg's shoulder was a generic hotel picture hanging on the wall behind him, the same bland, unmemorable abstract print the world over. But there was a tiny detail that grabbed Bishop's attention; there was a reflection in the glass. Backwards and blurred, he could barely make out the digits. 11:11. Bishop's head pivoted around. The same green digits of the clock by the bedside table now said 11:25. He was only minutes behind.

Sprinting from the room, Bishop tucked his gun into the rear of his belt. Oleg had a head start, but not for long. Bishop hit the stairs and took them three at a time.

The state of the penthouse suite gave him the minutest semblance of hope. There was no body. Demir's intelligence stated there had been a 'drunk blonde girl'. There was no blood in the room, no sign of a struggle. It may have been naive optimism on his behalf, but Bishop believed there was a chance, however slim, that Astrid was still alive.

Bishop burst through the fire doors and into the night. He didn't stop running.

There were no cars on the deserted streets, let alone taxis. Most drivers had wisely chosen to go home and protect their livelihood. No taxi driver in their right mind would be taking fares when any street could be blocked off with a burning barricade or angry mob. Yet these were the same streets Bishop ran down.

Several times in five minutes, masked individuals had called out to him, most likely the local equivalent of, 'Oi, mate, where you think you're going?' A few had even chased him, but soon gave up, unable to match Bishop's relentless pace. He knew two things couldn't last, his speed and his luck. Sooner or later he'd need to rest and one or more masked hoods would take exception to him. Bishop didn't want either of those things. All he wanted to do was find Astrid.

The more his concentric circle search pattern expanded, the more hopeless it seemed. Other things confounded him on his hunt. Why would Oleg leave the relatively safe confines of the hotel? It was vulnerable, sure, but at least it was defendable. Perhaps Oleg had spied Bishop on the street and assumed a fully orchestrated attack was on its way. If that was the case, Oleg had no team of his own. That meant they were evenly matched. All Bishop had to do was find him.

Then he did.

Down a side street, opposite a flaming Mercedes, Bishop spotted a hulking figure with a bundle over his shoulder slink around the corner. The bundle had blonde hair.

Bishop drew his gun and closed in. A couple of members of a chanting, hooded group of youths yelled something in Bishop's direction but went suddenly quiet when Bishop waved the pistol at them.

Slowing as he neared the corner, Bishop steadied his breathing. He didn't feel too poorly after running the equivalent of a half marathon, but knew he needed to prepare his body for the confrontation to come. As slowly as he could, Bishop peered around the corner. The big Russian hadn't gotten far. His injuries slowed him; he limped awkwardly. The right leg of Oleg's jeans was torn and bloodied, as were his fists. He must have encountered trouble along the way. Unlike Bishop, he couldn't outrun it.

Stepping onto the street, Bishop raised his voice. "Put her down, Kong."

Reeling around, Oleg thrust his revolver at Bishop, his eyes wide. "You!... I... wait... I'm what?"

"I'm referring to King... have you never seen King Kong?"

Oleg frowned. "Yes, the giant ape that climbs the Twin Towers."

Bishop's shoulders sagged. "That's the only one you've seen?"

The Russian shrugged. "There are others?"

Bishop shook his head. "Yes, you're King Kong, the big stupid ape escaping with a defenceless blonde."

Tilting his head, Oleg looked at the woman on his shoulder and sighed. "Defenceless?"

"Fine. I knew as soon as I said the word how ridiculous it was." Bishop targeted his pistol at Oleg's heart. "Hand her over."

"Oh, okay, here you are." Oleg didn't move. After a moment he rolled his eyes. "Idiot." He scowled. "She is coming back to Russia to pay for her crimes."

That surprised Bishop. "You said you were here to kill her. I'm almost certain they were the exact words you used in Venice."

"My orders changed." It was clear Oleg was not altogether happy about the change to his mission parameters. He did his best to sound convincing. "We are not barbarians from your paranoid 1950s movies, Bishop. My people want to see justice done, just like you in the West profess to. Bringing this evil woman who is responsible for killing so many of our soldiers to justice, can you imagine? The SVR will be hailed, and so will our justice system, the efficient and effective government. It will be a triumph, and justice will have been served. They may even bring back capital punishment just for her."

There it was. It was a political move rather than a strategic one. Russia was on the precipice of a civil war. An espionage win on the world stage could help the government claw back some lost credibility. That didn't mean Oleg had to like it.

"I am walking out of here, Englishman." The gun in his hand was rock-steady. "You need to go back to your little life of tea and crumpets and cricket and forming orderly queues and whatever else you English do. You are done here, Bishop."

In response, Bishop pulled back the hammer of his pistol. "I hate to tell you, but I'm not going anywhere."

The two men stared one another down. Neither flinched. Neither would back down. It was a Mexican standoff.

Oleg had been dealt the tougher hand. Astrid over his shoulder would be weighing him down, especially given his injured ribs. Worse, his bloody leg made him unstable, even without the extra mass. He was a tough bastard though. His hand didn't shake, his eyes were clear and cold.

Down the barrel of a gun, the stalemate continued.

A group of five protesters with black scarves covering the lower part of their faces jogged past on the opposite side of the street. The youth at the head of the pack slowed, pointed at the deadly impasse across the street and mumbled something to his comrades. All five approached slowly.

The lead youth tilted his head. "Burada neler oluyor?"

When neither spy moved a muscle, he raised his voice. "Burada neler oluyor, Erkekler?"

Two of their number held planks of wood and pounded them in their hands menacingly. The group circled Bishop and Oleg, metres away. Soon they started shouting random phrases, the tone increasingly threatening. If the gang decided to attack while each spy was unable to move in fear of the other firing, both would lose. The situation was spiralling out of control and Bishop was running out of options.

As if reading his mind, Oleg hefted his eyebrow. It was only a few millimetres, the tiniest of gestures, but the sentiment was as loud as a jet engine. Bishop gave the smallest of nods in return.

At the exact same moment, both Bishop and Oleg turned on the mob and fired. The bullets went over the youths' heads, but the shock was enough to scatter them. They scrambled over one another, bolting up the street and out of sight.

"Thank you." Oleg sighed as he turned to Bishop. "Now perhaps we could—"

Bishop shot Oleg in his good leg. The big man crumbled. The weight of Astrid over his shoulder forced him to collapse, and his hurried counter shot was wide and sloppy. Bishop rushed in and kicked his pistol away, and the unarmed Russian grunted in anger.

"Again? Why the leg?" Oleg slammed his head against the concrete in frustration. "Why always the leg? You will die for this, you Ублюдок!"

Ignoring the SVR agent, Bishop gently lifted Astrid's head, which was resting on Oleg's thick thigh, and brushed the hair from her face. Checking her pulse, he sighed in relief. She was alive.

Ice in his veins, Bishop turned to Oleg. "If she was

dead the next bullet would have gone through your heart."

He was close to Oleg, but Bishop's gun was steady. The Russian knew he wouldn't hesitate to use it. Bishop had to get Astrid away from Oleg as soon as he could. The situation was far from safe.

"She is the enemy!" Oleg screamed, his face crimson. "Why do you protect the enemy?"

It was a question Bishop couldn't answer, not now—perhaps not ever. He stared down at Astrid's face and wished he could respond with logic. Everything he'd ever stood for, upheld and fought for, went against the reason he was on that filthy street. Yet he wouldn't have been anywhere else in the world.

Eyelids fluttering, Astrid groaned. Slowly, life returned to her angelic features. Her eyes focused on Bishop's face and she gave him a sluggish but vibrant grin.

"Hey, pretty boy." Her tongue roamed her mouth. "Did we have a big night? Can't remember it. Which is a shame. We on that tropical island yet?"

Bishop spoke quietly. "I'm working on it."

Oleg groaned, his eyes were like molten steel. "You can't win."

Bishop shrugged. "Sometimes I can."

"No." Oleg sucked in air through his teeth. "This time you can not."

Fast as lightning, Oleg's hand darted to Bishop's ankle. His holster, to be exact. Before Bishop could react, Oleg had the Double Tap derringer in his hand and had fired twice.

The cold night air froze. The sound of the gunshots echoed through the empty streets.

Bishop stumbled backwards in shock, unable to breathe.

The two shots Oleg had fired were at Astrid's face. The burst of blood and matter coated Bishop. Oleg pulled the trigger again, but nothing happened; its armaments of death spent.

Bishop frantically pulled Astrid to him in the desperate hope that she'd survived. It was futile. Her face and her life had been blown away. The gruesome carnage put an end to any hope that she'd miraculously evaded death's grim hand. Astrid Spencer was gone.

Limbs like lead, Bishop aimed the pistol at Oleg. With a primal scream of anger, he fired, emptying his entire clip.

Collapsing in a heap, Bishop wailed like he never had before. His empty weapon dropped from his numb hand. His insides had been cleaved from him, there was nothing left.

"You done, Englishman?"

Bishop blinked at the Russian. All his bullets had been aimed to come close but never to hit the big man. As much as Bishop wanted him dead, he knew Oleg had been performing his duty, something Bishop had wholly failed to do.

It didn't mean he didn't want the man dead.

Oleg looked from the dead body, the prize his government had wanted to bring to justice, the woman who had murdered so many of his compatriots. He did not smile. Oleg took no pleasure in her death.

The SVR agent looked from Astrid to his bloodied leg and then to Bishop. "We will meet again, but I cannot say I will spare your life next time."

Bishop rose and brushed himself off, taking one last glance at the body of the woman he had risked so much for.

"I really don't give a fuck."

Bishop walked into the still night.

# EPILOGUE

He stepped out of the elevator and into the hall. The corridors were much like any other office building. Nothing distinguished; the plain off-white walls could have been in any modern place of business. Only those who walked the halls knew their place of work was different than most. The decisions made within this particular building carried enormous weight. Everyone who walked the MI6 halls knew their decisions, or lack thereof, could affect the lives of millions. Or one.

On his return to London, Bishop had received no reprimand, no disciplinary action. He suspected the grace period wouldn't last. At least, he believed it was a grace period. He hadn't caught up with Bridgeman or Fitzherbert yet; he only hoped they hadn't lied on his behalf. He already had so much on his conscience.

Bishop had undergone all the requisite physical and mental assessments MI6 could throw at him. He had passed every one. The doctors advised he was fit for duty once more. He wasn't as certain as they were.

Not sure he'd ever been more exhausted, Bishop forced his drained body to place one foot in front of the other. After ensuring the halls were empty, he placed a hand on the wall for stability. Closing his eyes for the briefest of moments, he snapped them open again. This was the reason he'd been unable to sleep. Every time he closed his eyes he saw the prone Astrid lying on the filthy street, her once-beautiful face a bloody pulp. Bishop shook his head violently to dislodge the image. He knew it wouldn't work. It hadn't worked the last ten thousand times, why would this one be any different?

He straightened, doing his best to portray the outward impression of control, and walked forward. It was the only thing he could do. Anything less would end in entropy and death. As painful as it was, he had to keep moving.

Astrid must have seen the fracture in his soul, a tiny sliver, enough to believe she had seen the real Bishop. Maybe she had. Stupidly, he'd allowed her through the fissure. That was his undoing. He let her in and it had cost Astrid her life.

He would never make the same mistake again, Bishop vowed. He would never allow a woman to get close to him again. Tessa, Astrid, it didn't matter. He could never allow a woman to see the real him. He'd forge a new man, a colder, more aloof Bishop.

It was ludicrous to believe he'd never be involved with another woman again, that was crazy talk, but it would be on his terms. One-night stands; no commitments, no emotional entanglements. He'd forge an impenetrable layer of heartlessness and indifference. He would become a cad—even more than he had already been. His defences would be absolute. He just had to perfect them.

He needed time. One thing was certain, he wouldn't go near a woman of any type for a long time. He needed space. He needed to heal. He needed to perfect his new impenetrable shell.

Bishop strode into Paul's office without knocking. His boss was hunched over a computer, teacup in hand.

His superior didn't glance up. "I heard a nasty rumour you'd survived."

"You know me, always eager to disappoint."

Paul turned and smiled. "Good to see you, Charles."

"Good to be seen."

Paul took in Bishop standing in the centre of his office. "Is it done?"

Bishop placed a bottle of Glenfarclas 40-Year-Old on the desk. He strode to Paul's wet bar, extracted a couple of crystal glasses and returned to pour two generous drinks.

Handing one to Paul, Bishop was mute. Paul nodded his thanks.

From Paul's perspective, the mission was complete. Yousef Sharif was safe and where he needed to be. The capture of the two Pugliese siblings was the cherry on top. Astrid Spencer and her illegal Kali network had been eliminated. It was unfortunate that Lanaway's life had been lost in the line of duty, but his killer had paid for her crime. She would never cause international strife, never be responsible for any more loss of life. For Paul, it was all very clean.

It was the opposite for his subordinate. But that was a burden he would shoulder alone.

There was one more item Bishop took away from this mission. If he ever saw Oleg again, he would kill the son-of-a-bitch. There was no gloating on the Russian's side. To his credit, he seemed to take no pleasure in Astrid's demise, not that it mattered. If Bishop ever crossed paths with Oleg there would be a reckoning, and only one of them would be left standing.

Motioning for Bishop to sit, Paul tapped the desk. "Doc Ellroy says you're fit for duty."

"So I hear."

Paul nodded. Behind his desk, he squirmed uncomfortably. It was an unusual move for the man. He hesitated, then forged on. "I have a… a task for you."

Bishop tilted his head and smirked. Paul's coyness was intriguing. "A task? I don't believe you've given me a *task* before."

"Ah, yes, well, that's because this one isn't strictly… it's more of a favour than a task, I suppose. One you're welcome to decline, though, ah, I rather hope you won't." Paul scratched the back of his neck, his face growing pink.

"What's the task, Paul?"

He tugged at his collar. "I need you to go see a woman."

Bishop blinked. "A woman?"

"You're familiar with the sex?"

"I've heard of them, certainly. Even seen pictures in magazines."

"Well, this task's rather delicate, you see. If you tilted your head sideways and squinted you could call it official, but I'd have a hard time justifying it to the Minister, let me tell you. I just… it's, ah."

Bishop smiled again. "Spit it out, old friend."

The last word made Paul look up and relax. It seemed to instil him with confidence. "I need you to speak to a friend of mine. Well, more Nancy's friend than mine… bugger it, no, she's a good friend of mine too. She's, ah, she's fallen in with… let's just say, she needs to be put right. I can't do it or she'll know who I work for. I need someone…"

"Devilishly handsome?"

"Dispensable." Paul pursed his lips.

"Funny man." Bishop finally felt the minutest part of him relax. "This friend of yours, she doesn't know you work for MI6?"

"Good lord, Nancy doesn't even know, and I trust my good lady wife more than anyone on the planet."

"Thank you very much."

"You're most welcome." Paul sipped his whiskey. "No, the young lady in question believes I work for the Treasury. I'm keen for that to remain the case. So, I need someone who is of the utmost professionalism, possessing supreme surreptitiousness and propriety."

"You need someone sneaky."

Paul tapped his nose. "Precisely."

"I see. And what am I meant to do, exactly?"

"Well, while this girl can be crass, drink like a fish and can be a royal pain the arse, she has one of the biggest hearts I've ever known. And that, they say, is the rub. She's gotten herself involved with someone supremely powerful and she doesn't quite understand that his intentions for her, or indeed anyone, are not as honourable as she thinks. I need someone to dissuade her from having anything to do with the man, you see."

"You want me to tell someone not to date someone else?" Bishop screwed up his face. "Is that it?"

It didn't sound like something Bishop would touch with a ten-foot barge pole. But then Paul told him who the man was. That changed everything.

"Oh, Jesus fuck."

Paul smiled. "That sounds like something she'd say. She has quite the potty mouth, I'm afraid. Oh, and one last thing. Granted, the poor girl had little say in it, but she is inflicted with the most grievous condition."

"Which is?"

"She's Australian."

"Good lord."

"I know. Try not to hold that against her; I do my best not to."

It seemed Bishop was leaping into the exact scenario he'd vowed to avoid not five minutes before. But he owed Paul so much, this small task surely wouldn't cause him any trouble.

"This friend of yours, does she have a name?"

"She does." Paul raised an eyebrow. "It's Eva Destruction."

THE END

# VIP BOOK CLUB

To be the first to find out when new novels arrive and to win prizes and get free stuff (who doesn't like free stuff?), sign up for my VIP Book Club at:

https://davesinclair.com.au/newsletter/

# EVA DESTRUCTION

Hey there,

So ends the Bishop story, or does it?

If you've enjoyed the Bishop novels, did you know they lead directly into my first series – *Eva Destruction*. That's right, the Bishop novels are the prequel to the next big adventure…

**Meet Eva Destruction, the only thing quicker than her mouth is her talent for getting into trouble –** *The Eva Destruction Collection.*

It's true she's always had an eye for a bad boy, but when she falls for billionaire super-villain Harry Lancing, it seems that even Eva may have bitten off more than she can chew.

As the odds begin to stack up in Lancing's favour, the fate of the world lies in Eva's hands. Luckily for the world, Eva Destruction isn't the type of girl to let a super-villain ex-boyfriend with a massive ego, unlimited resources, and his own secret island, get the better of her. With the charming, but enigmatic fellow spy Bishop by her side, Eva will have her hands full.

A trilogy in four parts, *The Eva Destruction Collection* combines three full exhilarating Eva Destruction novels and one Eva Destruction novella in an explosive collection.

Well over 1000 pages of pedal-to-the-metal action and whip-smart dialogue, this box set will keep you reading well into the night.

Here's what others have said about Eva's adventures:

"This book is what would happen if James Bond and Stephanie Plum had a baby. Fast moving action packed romp. I loved it. It's fun, it's funny, it's clever. I want a movie of this now. Brilliant."

"This was such an exciting and fun read. I loved every page and did not want it to end. I want more Eva Destruction NOW! Please?"

"This was a whole lot of fun! With a kickass heroine and good blend of action, intrigue and romance, it kept me engaged from start to finish. It even kept me reading late into the night, which says something. It also made me laugh! Thoroughly enjoyed."
I hope you enjoy, and thanks for your support!

Dave Sinclair

P.S. If you enjoyed the read, please consider leaving a review. It really helps a lot.

P.P.S. If you want to keep in touch, you can sign up to my VIP Book Club newsletter at https://davesinclair.com.au/newsletter/

# ABOUT DAVE SINCLAIR

Dave Sinclair is a novelist, a screenwriter and a really excellent parallel parker.

He lives in Melbourne, Australia with his two crazy daughters. He's also an award-winning filmmaker, a title that sounds far more impressive than it really is. He won a best comedy screenplay and cinematography award for a short film he wrote and directed, though at the time he didn't really know what cinematography was. A completed screenplay is currently doing the rounds.

Dave's overflowing bookshelves include many works by Douglas Adams, P.G. Wodehouse, Dashiell Hammett, Raymond Chandler, Janet Evanovich, Ian Fleming, Zadie Smith and John le Carré.

To find out more, you can stalk Dave at his semi-reputable website: https://davesinclair.com.au

# ACKNOWLEDGMENTS

This book just flew. From page one it had a life of its own. It's like Bishop needed his story told and he wouldn't let up until I wrote The End. It was a little sad to finish this trilogy as I was having an absolute blast. The story closed out how I envisaged it when I first began, and it dovetailed into the Eva books just as I'd hoped. Is this the end of Bishop? Oh, I don't think so! I think there's plenty more adventures to be had.

Now for the acknowledgements!

Since finishing this book and writing the acknowledgements, something amazing happened. My beautiful and amazing fiancée became my wife. Kristi, thank you for your support, encouragement and belief in me. It means the world. All the love.

To my crazy girls, Quinn and Esther, a HUGE thank you for supporting your dad and continuing to be my cheer squad. I adore that you've taken on your love of reading from me, although it might be a few years before you read these particular books…

As always, thanks to the G-Mob, my writing tribe. The G-Mob are amazing writers and even better friends.

Craig, Justin, Luke, Nathan, Steve, Amanda and Amanda, thank you for your support, encouragement and laughs.

And to my sis, Alli, thank you for always being supportive. Even after you dedicate your book to me and I dedicate mine to the cat. Thanks for always being there. Check out her novels – http://allisinclair.com. We won't stop writing until our mum's coffee table buckles under the weight of all our books.

As always, a big thank you to my editor Vanessa Lanaway for her talented and speedy work. She really does make me sound like I know what I'm doing.

Thanks to Amanda Pillar (a member of the G-Mob and a great writer) who designed all the Bishop covers. Check out her cover work here – https://www.smokinghotcovers.com/

There were two sneaky mentions within this novel. One, David Lanaway (remember that jerk?), was named after a real-life lovely member of my newsletter recipients. He won a competition to have his name in this novel. I'm sure he's nowhere near the jerk the other David Lanaway was. Probably. And to Penelope Fitzherbert, she won having her name in the novel by being the successful bidder on a Twitter auction. All proceeds went to the Australian firefighters who did an amazing job putting their lives at risk during the recent devastating bushfires.

And to my fabulous Book Ninjas who receive an advance copy of my novels – thank you for the amazing feedback! You guys are brilliant.

(Phew, almost there!) And don't be afraid to reach out on Facebook, Twitter, Instagram. It's always great to hear from readers. You can stalk me at all these semi-reputable places:

www.davesinclair.com.au